"You feel you're one of them? One of the *Englisch*?"

"Sometimes." Abigail looked defensive. "I can hardly help it. I spent my adult years among them. How else did you expect me to feel?" She plucked at her dress. "Outside appearances and inside feelings are two different things."

For a brief moment, Benjamin felt sorry for her. She was obviously not comfortable in her own skin. "You're torn," he murmured.

"Of course I'm torn. You would be, too, in my position."

"*Ja*, maybe, except I wouldn't have put myself in your position." The moment the words were out of his mouth, he felt ashamed. He slapped a hand to his forehead. "*Ach*, that was rude. I'm sorry."

His apology seemed to deflate her defensiveness. Her smile was tinged with sadness. "Let's just say I'm taking this opportunity to help *Mamm* after her surgery to do a lot of thinking."

"That's a start," he commented.

"A start?" she responded. "Of what?"

"The start of transforming you back into an Amish woman."

Living on a remote self-sufficient homestead in North Idaho, **Patrice Lewis** is a Christian wife, mother, author, blogger, columnist and speaker. She has practiced and written about rural subjects for almost thirty years. When she isn't writing, Patrice enjoys self-sufficiency projects, such as animal husbandry, small-scale dairy production, gardening, food preservation and canning, and homeschooling. She and her husband have been married since 1990 and have two daughters.

Books by Patrice Lewis

Love Inspired

The Amish Newcomer
Amish Baby Lessons
Her Path to Redemption
The Amish Animal Doctor

Visit the Author Profile page at LoveInspired.com.

The Amish
Animal Doctor

Patrice Lewis

LOVE INSPIRED
INSPIRATIONAL ROMANCE

LOVE INSPIRED®
INSPIRATIONAL ROMANCE

PLEASE RECYCLE
THIS PRODUCT IS RECYCLABLE

Recycling programs
for this product may
not exist in your area.

ISBN-13: 978-1-335-56761-1

The Amish Animal Doctor

Copyright © 2022 by Patrice Lewis

This edition published by arrangement with Harlequin Books S.A.

For questions and comments about the quality of this book, please contact us
at CustomerService@Harlequin.com.

Love Inspired
22 Adelaide St. West, 41st Floor
Toronto, Ontario M5H 4E3, Canada
www.LoveInspired.com

Printed in U.S.A.

For as we have many members in one body, and all members have not the same office: So we, being many, are one body in Christ, and every one members one of another. Having then gifts differing according to the grace that is given to us.

—*Romans* 12:4–6

To my husband and daughters,
my greatest earthly joy.

To Jesus, for His redeeming grace.

To God, who has blessed me
more than I could possibly deserve.

Chapter One

Dimly, through the fog of sleep, Abigail Mast heard a pounding at the front door.

She opened her eyes into the dark room and smelled the cool summer night through her open screened window. A glimmer of pale light had barely seeped over the eastern horizon. It was dawn, but the nighttime frogs and crickets still chirped. She heard the deep hoot of great horned owls from the nearby forest that surrounded her mother's rental cottage, a few miles outside the tiny town of Pierce, Montana.

The pounding on the door came again. From the other bedroom, Abigail heard her mother's weakened call. "Abigail? *Liebling*, someone is at the door."

"*Ja, Mamm.* I'll see who it is." Abigail pushed back the blanket, swung her feet to the floor and snatched a bathrobe to cover her night-gown. She slid her feet into slippers and hurried into the dark living room, yawning. She'd finished nearly a week of hard driving, coming all the way from Indiana, and had only made it in around midnight. Now, this…

On the porch, barely visible in the fading night, appeared the figure of a disheveled man. He wore no hat, his shirt was untucked and his features were too shadowed to see. He breathed hard, as if he'd been running…or carrying a heavy load. "Are you Esther Mast's daughter Abigail?" he asked, panting.

"Ja," she replied.

"I understand you're a veterinarian—is that true?"

"Ja, but—"

"I have a dog with a broken leg." He gestured toward the yard. "Can you help her?"

Abigail peered through the gray dawn light and saw a huge bundle of white fur lying on the grass. But rather than approaching the animal, she drew her robe tighter around her, as if to shield herself from the man's plea. "There is a vet clinic in town."

"It's too far away and it would hurt the dog to transport her there by buggy. Besides…" A note of bitterness crept into his voice. "They're *Englisch*."

Well, of course they are, she thought, but didn't say it out loud. Instead she fought the waves of sickening insecurity that had plagued her professional judgment since she had nearly lost a prized dog because of her ineptness last month.

"Bitte?" the man asked again. "Please?"

From the yard, Abigail heard the dog whimper in pain, and in that moment she knew she had no choice. *Gott* had given her the gift of healing animals. She could not deny a creature in pain.

"I have very few vet supplies with me," she explained. "But I'll do what I can. Bring her onto the porch and let me get what I have."

He nodded and turned. Abigail retreated into the house and dragged out her truck of veterinarian supplies, which she'd had the forethought to bring with her.

"Who is it?" called her mother.

"I don't know, but he has a dog with a broken leg," she called back. "Stay there, *Mamm*, I'll just be on the front porch."

"Ja, gut."

The man had carried the dog to the porch and now squatted down, smoothing the animal's fur.

Abigail tried to forget she was attired in nightclothes. She was conscious that her hair was not properly tucked up under a *kapp*, but hung in a long loose braid to her waist. Instead, she focused with laser intensity, as she always did, to help an animal in need. She kneeled down and touched the injured foreleg. "How did she break it?"

"I don't know. I heard her cry from the field, where she guards my cows. I don't think she tussled with a coyote or a wolf—she'd have bite marks if she did."

"Is she a Great Pyrenees?"

"*Ja.* A livestock guardian."

Abigail noticed something, and ran a hand over the dog's belly. "And she's pregnant."

"*Ja.* The puppies are due in a month."

She bit her lip. "I don't have an X-ray machine," she warned him. "I'm just running on instinct. Will you trust me?"

"Of course. Do what you can."

Knowing the animal might bite her from sheer pain, Abigail rummaged among her supplies and drew out a muzzle, which she expertly wrapped around the dog's snout before the animal could object. But in the dim light, the dog's deep brown eyes—though tinged with pain—only looked at her with calmness.

"*Ach,*" breathed the man. "You've a good touch with animals. I see she trusts you already."

"My gift from *Gott*," Abigail muttered. Without picking up the limb, she gently probed the animal's foreleg. "Ulna isn't broken, but the radius is snapped. Clean break. No skin penetration. Perhaps a cow stepped on her leg, or kicked her. Can't tell if there are bone fragments, but—" She pressed gently and the dog whimpered.

The man continued to bury his hands in the dog's thick white neck fur, soothing and restraining at the same time.

Abigail looked up at him. "I'm going to take a chance and cast her leg, but I strongly recommend you bring her to the vet clinic in town for X-rays to confirm there are no bone fragments. I can't tell for certain, but the break feels very clean. If I had all the tools at my disposal, I'd give her an external fixator for the fracture, where I put pins through the skin and into the bone. That would allow the fracture to heal while letting her use her leg in a normal way. But about all I can do right now, with what supplies I have here, is to cast the leg, then fit her with a cone around her neck so she can't chew at the cast."

"*Ja*, please. Anything."

Abigail nodded, wondering why he wouldn't simply take the animal to town, where the vets could provide the best of care. Besides, a shock big enough to fracture a leg bone might have caused damage to other organs as well…and this dog was pregnant.

She sighed. "All right, I'll do my best."

For the next half hour, as the sky lightened and dawn broke, Abigail treated the dog's leg. In the end, the cast was in place—it was damp but firm—and she was able to find a plastic cone to fit around the dog's neck.

She also took the opportunity to examine the man unobtrusively. His dark hair was curly and his beardless chin had a bit of stubble on it, probably from his all-night vigil. But the laugh lines at the corners of his dark blue eyes—shadowed from lack of sleep—showed he had good humor, and his gentle touch with his dog indicated a caring disposition. He also looked familiar somehow.

"There. That's the best I can do," she said at last. "Let's get her up." She stood up, stretching her cramped limbs.

The man also stood, grunting a bit as he unfolded himself from his position restraining the dog on the porch. The enormous Pyrenees rolled onto her belly and tried to sniff at the cast, but the plastic cone prevented her. She wagged her tail when Abigail bent to pet her. "What a beauty," she crooned.

"Her name is Lydia. She's my favorite dog.

Ach, there's a *gut* girl..." he added, as the dog gingerly got to her feet. She balanced herself on three legs and lightly touched the paw of the injured leg onto the ground as if testing it.

Abigail stroked the animal's long fur. "I'll give you some pain pills for her. I haven't spent much time around Pyrenees. There aren't so many predators in Indiana, where I worked, so most farmers didn't have guardians for their herds. She's gorgeous."

"We have a lot of predators out here—cougars and coyotes and bears and wolves. I lost a calf my first year here, but since getting Pyrenees, my cows have been safe. Now everyone else in church wants some, too, for their herds." He held out his hand. "I'm Benjamin Troyer, by the way. I remember you from when we both lived in Grand Creek."

Abigail shook his hand, peering at him more closely. "Benjamin! Of course. I remember you now. Goodness, it's been a long time. Last I heard you were..." She trailed off and had to restrain herself from smacking her forehead.

Last she heard, he'd been courting a pretty young woman named Barbara, but his beardless face stopped her from saying anything. If he'd married the woman, he would have grown a beard. She felt herself blush at nearly bringing up what could be an embarrassing topic.

"Wh-what brings you to Montana?" she stuttered instead, hoping he hadn't noticed her blunder.

"Land prices, what else?" he replied. "Farmland in Indiana was getting scarce and expensive, as you well know. That's why so many church members decided to up and move here to Pierce, to start a new church and some new farms."

"*Ja.* My mother, she wanted a bit of an adventure after *Daed* passed away five years ago."

"I think that was the motivation for quite a number of people. Your *mamm*, she rents this house from me."

"Oh! So you own all this?" She gestured across the porch, toward the fields and forests around them.

"*Ja.* I have sixty acres, and it came with a number of outbuildings, as you can see. This one was outfitted as a guest house, and Esther said it's all she needed."

"*Mamm* didn't expect her hip to give out as quickly as it did." Abigail stroked the dog's flank. "I'm just glad I had a chance to come out here and help her recuperate after her surgery."

"She's been talking of little else than your

visit. The whole church knows you're here to take care of her."

Abigail wasn't sure she liked being the subject of church gossip, but she supposed it was natural. She was an oddity. Most Amish women didn't disappear from the community for ten years to obtain a veterinarian degree.

Whether she would remain in the community was still a question she couldn't answer. Her excuse to travel to Montana was to help her mother recover from surgery. But her unspoken reason was to make an extraordinarily difficult decision—whether to return to her childhood faith, or remain forever in the *Englisch* world.

"Well…" She retied her bathrobe more firmly around her middle. "I hope you don't expect me to act like a veterinarian while I'm here. I—I don't think I'm that skilled. That's another reason you should bring this dog to someone more competent than I am." A note of bitterness crept into her voice. "After all, that's why I'm back here taking care of my mother. I couldn't hack it in the *Englisch* world."

Benjamin was startled by the tone of self-recrimination in Abigail's voice. He'd just watched her set Lydia's leg with gentleness and precision, yet she thought she was inept? There was a story there. He wondered why he cared.

He remembered her as a child back in Indiana. Consumed as he was by the woman he was courting, he recalled Abigail as an idealistic kid, obsessed with animals and determined to help them no matter what. He hardly noticed when she'd left to go to college, because he was too busy courting Barbara. And then... Barbara was gone, sucked into the *Englisch* world, lured by its brightness and glitter.

And then his beloved older sister had also left the Amish to become a nurse. Benjamin had a big reason to distrust the *Englisch* world and all its temptations, especially with the women he loved.

Now here was that formerly gawky kid he remembered, all grown up. Abigail's thick honey-colored braid hung to her waist. She had large chocolate-brown eyes, which were unusual among the Amish, and they gave her face a graceful beauty. She was a small woman, only a couple inches over five feet, but her size didn't hamper her skill.

But he was done with women who were in any way connected to the outside. While grateful for Abigail's competence with his dog, her very presence reminded him of the losses in his life, both with Barbara and with his sister.

"—these dogs?" she asked.

Benjamin blinked himself back to the present. "I'm sorry, what did you say?"

"I said, so you're breeding these dogs?"

"*Ja.* There's a huge demand right now, especially since I'm not the only one who has lost an animal to predators." He buried his hand in his dog's magnificent mane. "Lydia here, she and her mate guard my cows. This is her second litter, and every last puppy is already spoken for, however many she has. I'm thinking on getting a second female, more as a household pet, but which I can also breed. There are many farmers in our church whose livestock need protection."

He heard a voice from inside. Abigail cocked her head. "Excuse me, *Mamm* is calling."

"*Ja*, see how she's doing. I'm sorry to take so much of your time."

Abigail nodded and ducked inside. He was just starting to help Lydia down the porch steps when she reappeared. "*Mamm* asked me if you wanted coffee."

"Oh." He drew himself up. "*Ja*, sure."

"*Mamm* also said the dog is welcome inside. There's a comfortable mat she can rest on."

"*Danke.*"

He followed Abigail indoors and saw Esther, dressed in a bathrobe, seated at the table in the cheerful cream-and-sage kitchen. "*Guder mariye*, Esther. How are you feeling today?"

"I've felt better. Mighty glad Abigail is here to help me. I'm just sorry I can't cook for you."

He saw Abigail's eyebrows raise in surprise. "You've been cooking for him, *Mamm*?"

"*Ja.* It's part of my rent."

"I'm not much of a cook," Benjamin explained.

"*Ach*, I didn't know that. I'd be happy to help in that department. Um, excuse me." She glanced down at her bathrobe. "I should get dressed." She turned and disappeared.

"You look *gut* for being a week out of the hospital." Benjamin sat down opposite Esther and patted her hand.

"*Danke.* Things hurt right now, but I know I'll get better. Especially since my *boppli* is home." Esther's eyes took on a misty look of maternal love.

Benjamin chuckled. "You missed her that much?"

"*Ja*, of course. I've seen her very little since she left, and not at all since I moved here to Montana."

"How long will she stay?"

"I don't know." Esther's faraway look vanished and a troubled expression took its place.

"She told me she could stay about two months. I'm hoping she'll stay longer."

Benjamin was sorry he'd brought up the subject. Evidently there was a complication about Abigail's visit he knew nothing about. He rose and moved toward the wood cookstove. "I can at least manage coffee. Have you had any yet?"

"Nein." The older woman managed a rusty chuckle. "It was all I could do to hobble from my bed to this chair. I'm still learning to use the walker." She gestured toward the wheeled implement.

Benjamin added a stick of wood to the stove and put the coffee percolator on the burner. He paused, not sure where the coffee cups were. Then the bedroom door whisked open and Abigail emerged, properly dressed in a dark green dress with a black apron, and was pinning her *kapp* over her tucked-up hair. In his eyes, there was no prettier clothing for a woman. Or maybe it was the woman wearing them.

"Where do you keep the coffee cups?" he asked.

"I've no idea. I didn't get in until late last night." Abigail looked at her mother. "*Mamm?* Where will I find things?"

"Cups are in that cupboard over there." Esther pointed. "And I keep coffee in that can on the counter."

Benjamin returned to the kitchen table as Abigail bustled around, pulling together the beverage. Within a few minutes the percolator was boiling, and she poured out cups, placing them on the table with a jar of fresh milk and a bowl of sugar.

"Ah, *danke*." Benjamin took a sip. "It's been a long night."

"*Ja*, for all of us." He watched as she took a reverent sip of the beverage. "I woke *Mamm* up when I got in around…what, *Mamm*, midnight or so?"

"Something like that." Esther's eyes crinkled. "I know I was sound asleep."

"How did you get here?" Benjamin asked. "The nearest airport is in Missoula."

"I drove." She gestured behind the house. "My pickup truck is parked out back."

His eyes widened. "You can drive?"

"*Ja*. I've lived in the *Englisch* world long enough. I had no choice."

To Benjamin, it was another indicator that Abigail was not Amish, no matter how much she looked the part. She might have grown up into a beautiful woman, but he wasn't about to become interested in someone with both feet planted firmly elsewhere. To cover his dismay at that realization, he added, "It must have been a long drive from Indiana."

"It was. It took me five long days. But I had a large trunk of vet supplies I wanted to bring, as well as a fair amount of my household luggage, so it was more efficient than anything else. By the way, I owe you an apology. If I'd been thinking straight earlier, I would have offered to drive you and the dog into town to see the vet."

"I think you did a fine job." He looked over at Lydia, asleep on the mat, her cone flattened on the floor under her neck. "I think she's exhausted from the pain and stress, but you did a fine job with her."

"Oh, I almost forgot. Let me get you some pain medication for her." She stood up and went to the open trunk, which he could see held a variety of veterinary items. She rummaged around until she found a large bottle, which she brought back to the table. "I think two pills a day for a week should be enough." She poured some pills out on the table and counted them out. "*Mamm*, do you have something I can put these in?"

"I have some jars in the cupboard over there."

She fetched a small jar with a lid and transferred the pills to it, then pushed the jar toward him. "There you go."

"Danke." He picked up the jars and looked at the small pink pills. "That's quite a collection of supplies you have. Do you plan to open a clinic or something while you're here?"

He saw her face shutter. "No. I'm just here to help *Mamm* recuperate from surgery."

He didn't ask why she thought it was necessary to schlep a huge trunk of veterinarian supplies across the country if she was only here to help her mother for a couple of months. There were some undercurrents here he didn't understand, and frankly didn't want to.

"Well." He stood up. "In that case, I'd best get home. I have cows to milk and chickens to feed."

"Abigail can bring you some lunch later on," offered Esther.

He saw Abigail glance at him. *"Ja*, sure. I'll bring you some lunch, if that's the agreement between you and *Mamm*."

"Danke. And I can't tell you how grateful I am for setting Lydia's leg. Can she walk home, do you suppose, or shall I carry her?"

"How far away is your house?" Abigail asked.

"Just about a hundred yards, that way." He pointed.

"Do you want me to drive you back with the dog?"

That was the last thing he wanted. "No, I'll manage. If she can't walk, I'll carry her."

"She's a big dog to be carried!"

"I carried her here."

"Well, see if she can walk. Go slowly. If not, then try carrying her."

Benjamin coaxed his dog out of her sleep. The animal took a few shaky steps, but gained confidence as she moved across the room.

"I'll go slowly," he told Abigail. "*Vielen Dank* for everything."

He matched his pace with the hobbling dog, making sure not to go faster than she could manage. He found he was anxious to get out of the house, away from Abigail. She was entirely too attractive, and he had no intention of cultivating a personal interest in her.

After Barbara had left him high and dry and disappeared into the *Englisch* world, and after his sister had done the same thing, he had schooled himself to be alone. He had never courted another woman. He liked his solitude. He liked breeding his dogs. He liked his profession as a furniture craftsman. He liked his new home here in Montana. In short, he had built himself a solid, respectable life…alone.

He had his faith and his church community, and that was enough.

He didn't want to contemplate the alternative—what it might be like to *not* live alone.

Chapter Two

After Benjamin left, Esther said, "It's such a beautiful morning, let's go sit on the porch. We have a lot of catching up to do."

Abigail didn't have to be urged. She had arrived after dark and barely had a chance to glimpse anything of the stunning scenery around them. So she settled her mother as comfortably as possible into a rocking chair on the porch, then stood and looked out at the view.

Tall muscular mountains, capped with snow, rose above a rim of conifers to the west. Green meadows punctuated by groves of pine and fir trees surrounded them, spangled with flowers. A flock of garish black-and-white magpies, their exaggerated tails trailing behind, passed nearby. Scattered Jersey cows grazed in the pasture. She saw a huge white dog, doubtless

Lydia's mate, lying near a fence among the cows. The air was fresh and sweet.

Benjamin's house was, as he'd said, not more than a hundred yards away. It was a picturesque one-story log cabin with a broad front porch and smaller back porch.

"I wondered why you wanted to come to Montana," she ventured, "but I think I understand now. It's beautiful."

"*Ja*, I haven't had any regrets. It's wilder than Indiana, and somehow—lurking around corners—there's a tiny element of danger. Not from people, but from animals." Esther set her rocking chair in motion. "I like it here. I've seen moose and elk and bears and coyotes. Eva Hostetler—do you remember her? She was Eva Miller. She lives down the road now. She's sure she saw a couple of wolves last fall. I never thought I'd become an animal watcher like you, but it seems I have." Esther chuckled.

"I remember Eva. She's only two years older than me. I liked her." Abigail pulled another rocker over next to her mother and sat down with a sigh. "*Ach*, what a busy morning."

"And not much sleep for you last night—getting in around midnight and then being woken before dawn to fix the dog's leg."

"I'm just glad it was a clean break and an

easy fix, though I wonder why Benjamin refused to go to the clinic in town."

"He can be an odd duck, Benjamin."

"In what way?"

"He just seems to be a loner. Doesn't get out much, though I know he sells some dairy items to the Yoders' store in town. Otherwise he stays close to home."

"Is he baptized?"

"*Ja*, sure. He's been baptized for years."

"Why isn't he married?"

"I don't know. I gather something happened in his past, but he's never told me what it might be. He can be moody sometimes. I don't ask why, since it's none of my business. He's an easy man to cook for and he hardly charges me anything for rent, so it's a situation that's worked out well for us. I'm grateful to him."

"How did you come to rent this little house to begin with? It's cute." Abigail gestured upward, taking in the clapboard construction and modest porch, all painted a soft pale yellow.

"I was rooming with the bishop and his wife," explained Esther, "but when you're older like me, you need your own kitchen. Plus I had already made arrangements to make baked goods for the Yoders' store, and for that I needed room to work. Benjamin offered me this cottage and I accepted."

"It was the bishop's wife who took care of you just after you got out of the hospital, *ja*?"

"*Ja*. Lois, she's a *gut* woman. I was in sorry shape the first day or two, and she stayed with me day and night until yesterday, when she knew you were arriving."

"I'll have to do something to thank her." Abigail patted her mother's hand. "To be honest, I'm surprised you're up and about as much as you are. I thought a hip replacement would take longer to recover from."

"Actually, except for the pain of the surgery itself, I can already tell I'll be better soon. Stronger. The surgery was a *gut* thing." Esther paused. "As for this morning, you did a fine job with Benjamin's dog, *liebling*."

"She's a beautiful animal. If I had plans to stick around, I might be interested in having one of those puppies for myself. If any were available, that is."

"So you *don't* have plans to stick around?" inquired Esther.

Abigail winced. "I don't know yet, *Mamm*. I'm happy to be here for a couple months, but after that…"

"You have time to think about it. This little cottage is plenty big enough for us both for the time being. And the kitchen is big enough so once I'm back on my feet, I can continue baking for the Yoders."

"That's Abe and Mabel Yoder, *ja*? I remember they ran a little store in Indiana."

"*Ja*, the same couple. Two of their daughters came out here with them when the church moved, and they help run the store. Quite a number of us in the church contribute things to sell. The store is doing very well."

"Do you like making baked goods for the store?"

"It was a little hard being on my feet all day," Esther admitted. "But it gives me a nice bit of income and makes me feel useful. I can make things at home and bring them to the bakery. It's a nice chance to meet some of the *Englischer* in town, too. As a new church, we need to make sure we contribute to the community and are helpful."

"Are you going to make things for the bakery again?"

"*Ja*, as soon as I can." Esther waved a hand. "But that's in the future. You're here now. Tell me what happened, *liebling*. Why did you leave your job?"

Abigail knew this conversation was unavoidable. She shrugged with a nonchalance she did not feel. "You know pretty much all of it. I nearly lost a valuable dog because of my incompetence. Robert—the senior vet in the clinic where I worked—was able to save him, and then he chewed me out royally for messing up." What she didn't admit to her mother was how much she'd fancied herself in love with Robert. That little fantasy had come crashing down in a hurry. Instead, she added, "I was glad to take a leave of absence with the excuse of taking care of you."

"And that one experience with the dog was enough to make you doubt your gift? You've always had a way with animals, *lieb*. What is one mistake after years of success?"

Abigail didn't want to confess how much her lovelorn thoughts for Robert were entwined with her professional humiliation, so she just said, "I guess coming from my boss made it all the worse."

"Well, whatever the issue, I'm glad you're home for a bit. It's nice to have my *boppli* back."

Abigail smiled at the mother she'd missed so much. "It's nice to be back with you, *Mamm*. There hasn't been anyone to fuss over me since I left home ten years ago."

Esther chuckled. "But you're the one taking care of me, not the other way around."

"Just long enough for you to get better. I

know you, *Mamm*. Tell me the truth—you're just chafing to run a marathon, *ja*?"

Her *mamm* blushed slightly. "Maybe not a marathon, but I like cooking and baking. Are you up for doing that for both Benjamin and myself while you're here?"

"*Ja*, sure. That's what I'm here for, to make myself useful." She felt momentarily uneasy, like the feeling of inadequacy that had overcome her when Robert had yelled at her after her failure with the dog. "Should I have made him breakfast?"

Esther waved a hand. "You just set his dog's broken leg. I think that was enough. But normally what I do is bring lunch to his house. Sometimes he comes here for dinner, but not always. As I said, he often seems to prefer being alone."

"I don't have your skills in the kitchen, *Mamm*, especially since I've spent ten years not practicing enough. You'll have to guide me."

"That's fine. You've spent ten years acquiring different skills. Do you feel like you've developed your gift from *Gott*?"

Abigail silently blessed her mother. Esther was one of the few people who truly understood why she'd left the Amish, left the security of the church community. Abigail's love for animals wasn't just a girlish whimsy; it was her gift from *Gott* that she sought to develop by training as a veterinarian.

So she answered the question with the seriousness it deserved. "*Ja.* A part of me knows you're right, *Mamm.* That mistake with the dog was just one mistake, and thanks to Robert's skill, the animal fully recovered. I don't know why that one issue made me lack confidence in my own abilities, though."

"Well, now that you're here, perhaps you should look for a *hutband*."

Abigail felt herself blush. After her debacle with Robert, a husband was the last thing on her mind. She'd always known the senior veterinarian had a volatile temper, but he'd never directed it at her before. It was far more devastating than she was willing to admit, and it made her realize she wouldn't want a husband like that.

"I don't know, *Mamm*…"

"Do you want a *hutband* at all?" persisted Esther.

Abigail smiled at her mother's transparent interest in matchmaking. "I spent so many years wrapped up in animal medicine that I've hardly had a chance to think about it."

"Well, you're here now, *liebling*. Maybe you'll have time to put your mind to it."

"Maybe. But remember, *Mamm*, I'm not baptized. No Amish man will consider me seriously for that reason." She sighed. "It's like I'm straddling two worlds. It feels *gut* to dress this way again—" she smoothed her apron "—but it makes me feel like a fraud."

"*Gott* will direct your way," her mother said with a smile. "He's had His hand on you all these years you were in the *Englisch* world becoming a vet. Why would He abandon you now?"

"*Ja*, you're right. That's another thing I'm looking forward to while here—attending Sabbath services and being back among people of faith."

"Was it truly so bad, being away from the church?"

"*Nein*, not bad. Just…different. I got used to it because I had to, but it took a lot of adjustment…"

Esther tried to reposition herself in the porch chair, and Abigail saw her mother wince in pain. Instantly her own troubles were forgotten. "*Mamm*, I'm sorry. I'm so busy yammering about my own issues. Have you taken your pain medication this morning? Can I help you back into bed?"

Her mother's smile was a bit strained. "*Nein*, I haven't taken my pain pills yet. They're on the kitchen counter. As for going back to bed, I've spent enough time in there already. Instead help me back into the house and I'll guide you on making lunch. I have an idea of what Benjamin likes now."

Abigail helped her mother rise carefully, and she let the older woman lean on her heavily while she shuffled into the house. Remembering how active and vigorous her mother used to be made Abigail swallow hard. She supposed it was natural to dread the thought of parents getting older, but having lost her father already, she didn't want to think about losing her mother, too.

It made her wonder if returning to the *Englisch* world was worth the separation from her only remaining parent. Her father had passed away while she was gone. Her brothers and sisters were all married and living back in Indiana. She didn't want to think about not being here for her mother.

But once Esther had swallowed the pain medication and settled into a kitchen chair, she seemed to improve. "Are you used to cooking in a microwave now?" she teased.

Abigail chuckled. "I confess I never got used to that," she replied. "And it's nice to see a proper cookstove again. Okay, tell me what Benjamin likes to eat for lunch."

* * *

Benjamin ran a planer over a piece of oak. He squinted down the length of the wood and straightened up, satisfied.

Next to him on the shop floor, Lydia rested on a blanket. The dog was lying with her head down, the plastic cone flattened around her, with her leg cast a bit awkwardly to the side. But her eyes were alert, and that awful strain of pain was gone.

The dog suddenly jerked up her head and whined. Her tail swished and she tried to rise to her feet. Alarmed that she might hurt herself, Benjamin dropped his tools and started for the dog until he saw what had gotten the animal's attention. Abigail walked into the shop building, a covered basket in her hands.

His heart thumped unreasonably. "Oh, hello! I wasn't expecting you."

"I'm bringing you lunch in *Mamm*'s place." She placed the basket on a workbench, then kneeled down next to Lydia and stroked the dog. She chuckled. "I don't think I've ever seen such a beautiful dog."

Benjamin looked down at the woman crouching next to his pet. Her white *kapp* was tidy on her hair, and her black apron and green dress puddled around her knees as she fussed over the animal. "She certainly seems to like you. It's as if she understood you're the one who helped her."

"How has she been behaving? Any whimpering or acting agitated?" Gently, she probed the dog's injured leg around the cast.

"*Nein.* On the contrary, she's been calm and alert."

"I think it's safe to say she has no bone chips, then. A good, clean break." She ran her hand over the dog's belly, carefully feeling. "But you'll need to watch her when her due date gets near. I'd hate for her to have any complications when she whelps." She rose to her feet. "For the time being, I don't think it will be necessary for me to drive her to the vet clinic in town."

Mention of her vehicle was like a splash of cold water over Benjamin's face. It was a blatant reminder of the gulf between them—that Abigail was not Amish, despite her appearance. A little bit of his heart shriveled up inside him.

He strove to keep his voice level and dispassionate. "Have you considered opening a veterinary clinic for church members?"

Abigail looked startled. "*Nein*, of course not! What gave you that idea?"

He shrugged. "You might find a fair number of people might prefer to bring their animals to you than to the *Englisch* clinic in town."

"Why? What's wrong with the clinic in town?"

"N-nothing. It's just that…" He trailed off.

He saw Abigail's lips tighten. "It's because they're *Englisch*, is that it?"

"Maybe."

"Benjamin, this branch of our church is new in the area. We are the ambassadors of our faith. Yet you make it sound as if we plan to shun the local businesses, the very people who welcomed us to the area."

"*Ja*, I know." He turned away and fiddled with the planer. Not for anything would he admit his reasons for not wanting to associate with the local townspeople. Yet he was also aware of his hypocrisy, since a portion of his business was dependent on them.

He sighed. "You're right. I'm feeling un-accountably hostile toward the townspeople, for no *gut* reason. Everyone I've met so far has been kind and welcoming. Since I pro-vide products to the Yoders' store, I can hardly complain. And the bishop is working to make sure I conquer any hostility I may have."

He saw her startle. "The bishop? What can he do to make you less hostile toward the *Eng-lisch*?"

"He assigned me a task." He fingered a rough piece of wood on the worktable. "The town of Pierce has a yearly festival they call Mountain Days. It's a fairly big deal and attracts people from all over the region. This year the organizers came to the bishop and asked if we could put together a demonstration area featuring Amish skills and crafts. The bishop is anxious to make sure we establish the church community on *gut* terms with the town, so he agreed." He tightened his lips. "And guess who he put in charge of organizing it?"

"You?"

"*Ja*, me. He said it was because I don't have a wife and *kinner*, so I have fewer commitments than a family man might. But I agreed because I thought it might help my furniture-making business. I have some orders from church members, but not enough to keep me solvent. So I guess you could say I have an ulterior motive in taking on the task." He hoped that didn't sound too mercenary. In fact, he was barely making ends meet, and perhaps was pinning too much hope on the demo. "I plan to have a booth where I demonstrate how to construct a rocking chair. It's straightforward and I'm sure people will be interested, hopefully enough to order some furniture."

"I'm sure they will. The *Englisch* can be

very generous, and they like handmade things. Your business should flourish."

Benjamin didn't like how allied she seemed to be with the outside world. "Do you say that because you feel you're one of them? One of the *Englisch*?"

"Sometimes." She looked defensive. "I can hardly help it. I spent my adult years among them. How else did you expect me to feel?" She plucked at her dress. "Outside appearances and inside feelings are two different things."

For a brief moment, he felt sorry for her. She was obviously not comfortable in her own skin. "You're torn," he murmured.

"Of course I'm torn. You would be, too, in my position."

"*Ja*, maybe, except I wouldn't have *put* myself in your position in the first place." The moment the words were out of his mouth, he felt ashamed. He slapped a hand to his forehead. "*Ach*, that was rude. I'm sorry."

His apology seemed to deflate her defensiveness. Her smile was tinged with sadness. "Let's just say I'm taking this opportunity to help *Mamm* after her surgery to do a lot of thinking. I'm looking forward to attending Sabbath services. It wasn't always easy to attend church when I was in school or working."

"That's a start," he commented.

"A start?" she responded. "Of what?"

"The start of transforming you back into an Amish woman."

She shrank back a bit. "I *am* an Amish woman. No, I *was* an Amish woman…" She trailed off, then asked in a small voice, "Do I act *Englisch*? Am I so very different than I was?"

"I can't really say," he replied. "I hardly remembered you when we were *youngies*. I was too involved with—" He stopped. With great difficulty, he prevented himself from swiping a hand over his eyes. Of all people, why did he have to bring up Barbara? "Never mind," he muttered.

She didn't push or probe. Instead, she merely said, "Sounds like we both have regrets about our past."

"*Ja*, who doesn't?" To cover his blunder, he continued, "That's another question, I suppose. Which do you prefer, the *Englisch* or the Amish world?"

If he expected more defensiveness, he didn't get it. Instead she stared through the open workshop doors across the pasture, where cows were grazing. A large bird silently flew overhead. She tracked its trajectory with her eyes.

"Bald eagle." She pointed, then sighed. "I

don't know which I prefer yet. I spent eight years training to be a vet. I spent two years working in a clinic. I'm just home for a little while to help *Mamm*. I didn't realize…"

"Realize what?" he prompted, when she remained silent.

"Realize how much I missed my people." She glanced at him, then focused back on the pasture. "There's a lot to be said for the *Englisch* world. There are many things to do, many opportunities for everyone. But here, there's peace. There's faith. There's purpose. There's…well, there's *Gott*."

He was startled. "*Gott* is everywhere."

"*Ja*, of course. But it's not always easy to seek Him out. It's too easy to get distracted with other things…which is precisely why, of course, we Amish discourage higher education. And that, in a nutshell, is what I'm facing—the tug between my calling and my faith."

Calling. That's what she termed her veterinary training. He wanted to ask just what she meant by that, but it seemed too personal a subject.

Besides, for him there *was* no conflict. Faith always came first, job second. How could it be otherwise for her?

"I must get back to keep an eye on *Mamm*."

She turned to go, then spoke over her shoulder. "Are you coming for dinner? *Mamm* says you do, sometimes."

"If it's convenient, *ja*, I'd like to. What time?"

"How about sixish?"

"Sixish, then."

Without another word, she walked out the barn door.

He watched her slender figure as she headed back toward her mother's cottage. He could see her observing everything as she went—birds overhead, the cows in the field, his other dog, who was guarding the cows in his mate's absence. Animals always seemed to dominate her thoughts. He'd never met anyone with such an affinity for nonhuman creatures.

Abigail was dangerous. She was smart, compassionate, skilled…and pretty. She also had one foot firmly in the *Englisch* world. That alone was reason enough to leave her alone.

He'd lost two loved ones to the *Englisch* world. He stayed in fond touch with his sister Miriam—she was now a nurse—but Barbara was irrevocably lost to him. She had long ago married some *Englischer* and, as far as he knew, never regretted her decision to leave the church. How could he have been so blind as a younger man to fall for a woman intent on leaving?

And now here was Abigail, a woman he'd known since childhood but had never paid much attention to.

He drew his lips tight. Ten years since Barbara left—that's how long he'd been alone. Ten years of wondering if it was something he'd said or done to make her think the *Englisch* world was more attractive than the Amish community. Ten years of watching his cohorts pair off and marry and have children.

It was no accident that he'd volunteered to move with the church to Montana. Anything to leave behind his sour memories, and perhaps meet a woman who wouldn't mind a man still unmarried at age thirty.

But he'd met no such woman. Until now.

Chapter Three

Abigail took a bubbling dish of macaroni and cheese from the oven. As she placed it on a hot pad in the center of the table, she heard a knock at the door.

"That will be Benjamin." Esther tried to hoist herself out of a kitchen chair, but sank back down with a grunt of pain.

"Stay there, *Mamm*," ordered Abigail. "I'll let him in."

She padded in bare feet toward the front door of the cottage and whisked it open. He had a dusting of sawdust on his shirt. "*Gut'n owed*, Benjamin."

"*Gut'n owed.*" He removed his straw hat and sniffed the air. "Whatever's cooking smells *gut*."

"Macaroni and cheese. *Komm—Mamm* is in the kitchen." She turned and led the way through the house.

Benjamin entered the kitchen and hooked his hat over a chair back. "*Gut'n owed*, Esther. Any improvement today?"

"*Ja*, as long as I don't try to get up to let you in." The older woman smiled.

Abigail detected the faintest flirtatious note in her mother's voice, and it made her smile. Losing her husband had been hard on her mother, she knew. Whatever her reasons for moving to Montana, proximity to Benjamin seemed to have had a beneficial influence on the older woman.

"I brought your mail." Benjamin proffered several envelopes and a newspaper.

"*Ach, danke.*" Esther took the envelopes and scanned them. "Ah, how nice. A letter from my sister in Indiana. I'll read it after dinner."

"There's no mail service here?" inquired Abigail.

"*Nein*, not to this cabin. It all comes to my house," explained Benjamin. "Your *mamm*'s cabin is on my property, that's why."

After the silent blessing, Abigail dished out the food. Trying to make polite conversation, she asked Benjamin, "The furniture you make—do you sell it at the Yoders' store in town?"

"*Nein*." He paused to chew and swallow a bite. "Most of the furniture I make is for church

members. I've been too busy with that to expand elsewhere. What I sell at the Yoders' is
dairy products—cheese, yogurt, butter. You
might say dairy products are my evening job.
I'll be delivering some tomorrow, in fact."

"You mean you make furniture *and* dairy
products *and* breed Great Pyrenees?" She
stared. "You're a busy man, Benjamin."

He shrugged. "Right now my furniture business is slow, so dairy products fill my time
since—since I have no family."

She felt a shaft of curiosity about why he
was still unmarried, but it wasn't her place
to ask.

Before the pause could get awkward, Esther
piped up. "How is the planning going for the
Mountain Days event?"

"Slowly." Benjamin poked at his plate with,
Abigail thought, a trace of defensiveness. "I
sometimes wonder if I'm the right man for the
job."

"Maybe you should recruit my *boppli* here
to help you." Esther jerked her head toward
Abigail.

"Mamm," warned Abigail. "I'm here to help
you, remember?"

"Well, I don't need you to dance attendance
on me every hour of the day," Esther replied

with some asperity. "Helping with the Mountain Days event might be *gut* for you, *liebling.*"

Abigail was loath to commit herself. Instead, she changed the subject. "You said you were getting low on coffee, *Mamm*. I can go into town tomorrow and get some, if you like."

"*Ja, danke*. And I wouldn't mind some lemons, too, if they have some. Lemonade is a perfect summer drink."

"Since I'm bringing some things to the Yoders' store tomorrow, I can give you a lift," said Benjamin.

Abigail knew she couldn't suggest the use of her pickup instead of Benjamin's buggy. Driving a motorized vehicle would widen the chasm between herself and her church community. She needed to blend in as much as possible.

"*Danke*, that would be nice," she said instead. "What time?"

"Morning, probably. The Yoders' store opens at eight a.m., so if you want to come by around that time, we can drive in."

"*Ja, gut.*"

The next morning dawned fresh and clear. Abigail finished her short shopping list, gathered some money and kissed Esther on the cheek. "I doubt I'll be long," she said. "Don't run a marathon, *ja*?"

Her mother smiled at what was becoming a standing joke. "I promise."

Abigail made sure her *kapp* was firmly pinned in place, then set off on the short walk toward Benjamin's. A cheerful chorus of birdsong filled the cool air. She watched as a pair of evening grosbeaks swooped across her path before landing on a nearby conifer. The huge male Great Pyrenees guarding the cattle loped along the inside of the fence as she walked near.

"You're a beauty, do you know that?" she crooned as she reached through the fence wire and scratched the massive animal under the chin. "Your mate will be ready to join you again in a few weeks."

The dog pressed his ruff to the fence as she buried her hands in his coat. What an absolutely beautiful breed of dog, she thought. After a minute or two of bonding, she gave him a final pat and made her way toward Benjamin's cabin.

To her surprise, he was waiting for her on the front porch. "Elijah seems to like you," he observed.

Abigail blushed a bit at the thought of her quiet moment with the majestic dog being observed. "Is that the dog's name, Elijah? He's gorgeous. I don't know why this breed was never on my radar, but I really like them. How's Lydia?"

"Big and ungainly from carrying the puppies, but she's walking better. She hates that cone around her neck, though."

"I know, but we can't risk her gnawing off her cast before the bone is properly set. I'll remove the cone when she's whelping her puppies. Looks like you're ready to go," she added, glimpsing his horse already hitched to the buggy.

"*Ja*, I was just loading some items. Here, would you like to carry this basket of cheeses? I've got some jars of milk in the cooler."

Abigail helped him load the rest of his dairy products into the wagon, then climbed aboard the seat as he unhitched the horse. With a small jolt, he guided the animal onto the road.

"How far away is the town?" she asked.

"About three miles. Don't you remember? You drove through it a couple nights ago when you arrived."

"It was close to midnight and I was exhausted. It was just a dim blur to me."

"It won't take long to get there." He was silent a moment, then added, "I hope Esther didn't put you on the spot when she recommended you help with the Mountain Days event."

Abigail shrugged. "She did, a little. I think that's just the nature of mothers, ain't so? But if you need help, I suppose I can do something."

"I don't quite know what you could do."

She grew curious. "What exactly does your project entail? I mean, how are you going about convincing church members to make an appearance at this festival?"

"It's not quite as hard as you think," he replied. "First of all, the bishop is encouraging everyone to participate so we're viewed as co-operative members of the town. It's not like I'm getting a hostile reaction from any of the church members…"

"But you just don't want to do this, is that it?"

"It's outside my comfort zone." His expression suggested the admission was difficult. "But since I'm hoping it will give a boost to my business, I guess I don't mind."

"Well, I'm happy to help however I can, but since I've never done anything like this before, I don't know what to suggest."

"And it's not like you really know anyone anymore."

"*Ja*, there's that." She stared at the surrounding scenery. Benjamin's obvious observation depressed her for some reason. He was right. She hardly knew anyone anymore. "I've been away so long," she murmured.

"Does it bother you to be back?"

"*Nein*, it doesn't bother me. It's just…different. Being back in an Amish community is a big contrast. Everyone is more relaxed, less stressed here. I just have to get used to it."

"Since most of the people who moved here are ones you knew growing up, it won't take you long to slip back into the community."

"If I'm here long enough."

She saw him stiffen. "*Ja*, if you're here long enough. Look, there's the edge of town."

Abigail saw a simple grid of buildings. The road transitioned to pavement instead of gravel, and the horse's hooves clip-clopped on the asphalt with a bright sound. They came in from a side street through a series of quiet suburban homes. As they approached Main Street, she saw that it was lined with sturdy-looking older buildings—storefronts and offices—with more homes spreading out from the core. The town had a comfortable, settled air about it.

"How many people are in Pierce?" she asked.

"About twenty-five hundred." Benjamin waved at another buggy going the other direction. "Because the town is so isolated, it has a lot of the amenities people need—hardware store, grocery, a small hospital, things like that. There are now two buildings in town owned by church members. The Yoders opened their mercantile in a vacant storefront on Main Street and the city council was very glad to have them there. Apparently it's been vacant for quite some time." He pointed. "See? They even installed hitches for buggies."

Abigail saw a wide storefront with Yoder's Mercantile pained in a large sign across the awning. A Western-style rail had been installed for hitching horses. "What's the other building?"

"Eli and Anna Miller bought an old run-down building. I think it used to be a tiny hotel or something." He pointed. "They've spent the last year renovating it into a combination bed-and-breakfast, boardinghouse and meeting area. They're still working on it, but they've taken in a few early guests. They've also hosted two weddings for church members so far, since no one has a home big enough to handle it. That's another difference between settling here in Montana and our old place in Indiana—we have to adapt."

Abigail gazed at the Western-themed two-story building with a sign proclaiming Miller's Lodging.

"It looks *gut*. Do they live there?"

"No, because Eli won't give up his cows and they don't allow cows within city limits. So one of their sons lives there—do you remember Matthew Miller? He's doing the day-to-day work and getting used to the hospitality industry."

"It seems like the *Englisch* are very glad the church moved here," she observed.

"*Ja*, it seems that way. I gather the town was slowly dying, with many young people moving away to look for work. Having extra people means more revenue for the town."

"What's the main source of income for the area? It seems too forested for farming."

"Logging. That's the main source of revenue. That and cattle ranching, I believe."

He guided the horse toward the hitch in front of Yoder's Mercantile. Abigail climbed down from the buggy and reached in back for the basket of cheese while Benjamin hoisted the cooler filled with clanking jars of milk.

The storefront had a wide, covered wooden porch with stairs on one side and a ramp on the other. Outdoor buckets held colorful displays of cut flowers for sale. The windows were filled with attractive displays of merchandise—crafts, fabrics, antiques, quilts. "Looks like they sell a little of everything," she observed, glancing over the display. "Just like in Indiana."

"*Ja.* The *Englisch* love it." He turned and pushed the door open with his back, then held it while she slipped through.

In a moment she saw the store was arranged similarly to the Yoders' old store in Indiana, with a general mix of dry goods with a few select groceries, local produce and a dairy case. There was one new addition—a coffee area. Several older *Englisch* men in overalls and ball caps were sitting there with mugs and muffins, laughing and talking. A younger man sat before a laptop computer, earnestly typing, a mug of tea at his elbow. The smells of fresh bread and coffee filled the air.

"Nice," she observed, taking in the wooden flooring and gleaming glass display cases in a glance.

"*Ja*, the Yoders have always had a touch for retail. This place has become the logical spot to sell all the local Amish-made goods, but the Yoders also reached out to *Englisch* crafters and townspeople. The flowers out front, for example—they're grown by an *Englisch* family that lives outside of town. The store has to have electricity, of course, to legally sell dairy products and such. *Guder mariye*, Mabel," he added, lowering his ice chest to the floor.

Abigail turned and saw an older woman, plump and cheerful, in a black apron and pink dress.

"*Guder mariye*, Benjamin. And… Abigail? Abigail Mast? I heard you were visiting! *Welkom!*" Her face creased into a huge smile.

Abigail put her basket on the floor and embraced the woman. "*Danke!* It's *gut* to see you again!"

Mabel's warm greeting echoed through the store, and within moments several other Amish people crowded over to greet her. Abigail felt a warm flush at their enthusiasm as she renewed the acquaintances of several people from her youth. When the interest finally died down, she noticed a woman a few years older than her lingering in the background. Abigail did a double take. "Eva? Eva Miller?"

"*Ja!*" The woman catapulted forward and gave Abigail a hug. "But it's Eva Hostetler now. *Ach*, it's so good to see you!"

Benjamin lingered near Mabel, whose husband, Abe, bustled over to unload the jars of fresh milk. But as he helped unpack the cheese and butter, he watched as Abigail chattered with her long-lost friend. Eva Hostetler, he remembered, had grown up just a short distance away from Abigail when they were children in Indiana.

"It seems like she's fitting back in without a problem," Mabel murmured in his ear.

"*Ja.* But she says she doesn't know if she will stay yet." The words held more pathos than he would have liked.

Mabel gave him a sharp look before bending her head to write some information on her inventory sheet. Benjamin wanted to kick himself. The last thing he needed was some of the older women in the church playing matchmaker, especially with an unavailable woman. He would have to watch himself.

It took fifteen minutes for Mabel and Abe Yoder to log in the dairy products he'd brought, and Abigail spent the whole time talking with Eva Hostetler. He was certain Abigail could use a friend, so it pleased him to see her making a connection.

When his business was finished, he walked up to the two women. "*Guder mariye*, Eva. Abigail, I'm finished. Are you ready to go?"

"Oh, I forgot about my shopping. *Mamm* needs a few items. Eva, let's get together later on, *ja*?"

"*Ja, gut.* I'd like that." With a warm smile, the other woman walked away.

"I won't be long," Abigail told him. She

pulled a small piece of paper from her pocket. "Coffee, lemons, ginger and salt. That's all I need." She snatched a plastic basket from a stand and moved around the store, selecting her groceries.

Benjamin went outside to load the empty cooler and baskets into the buggy. By the time he was finished, Abigail came out carrying a paper bag. She climbed into the buggy as he unhitched the horse.

Her gaze tracked down the street and suddenly she went very still. "Look." She pointed.

Benjamin looked. The town's veterinary clinic was half a block from the Millers' bed-and-breakfast building. "What about it?"

"Nothing." She sat silent as he climbed into the seat and clucked to the horse. After a moment she added, "Except I wonder if I shouldn't go in and introduce myself."

He frowned. It was a reminder of the tug she felt toward the *Englisch* world. But he just said, "Are you hoping they'll hire you?"

"Nein!" She fell silent again as he directed his horse to mesh with moving traffic. *"Nein,"* she repeated more quietly. "I'm not licensed in Montana. They couldn't hire me."

"Do you want to get licensed?"

"I don't know. I don't think so. Oh, I don't

know!" The last words came out on a note of despair.

He glanced at her and saw a bleak expression on her face. "Abigail, are you going to be okay here in Montana? It seems you're torn up inside."

"I'll be okay." She straightened her shoulders. "*Mamm* needs me. Going into the vet clinic will only make things worse. I won't think about it."

He gave a noncommittal grunt and focused on directing the horse out of town. He sighed in relief when the road turned to gravel. In his mind, the end of pavement meant he was away from the *Englisch* world...including the vet clinic.

"*Mamm* told me this morning Eva is married," mused Abigail after a few minutes of comfortable silence. "It's not surprising since she's a bit older than I am. She looks happy. She said she has two children so far, a boy and a girl."

"She's, what, two years older than you?"

"*Ja.* If you remember, she lived only a short distance away from us in Indiana. We were never terribly close because I had friends nearer my own age, but it's awfully nice to reconnect with her. Our lives took such different directions," she added.

"Any regrets about the path you chose?"

"*Nein*. I suppose. I mean, I've given up a lot. Eva never gave up anything."

"But you've gained a lot, too. Eva never took the opportunities you did."

"The opportunity to do what? Leave behind everything that's comfortable and familiar?"

He was surprised at the bitter tone in her voice. "The opportunity to do something you always wanted to do," he reminded her.

"*Ja*, I know you're right." She took a deep breath. "There are just times I forget. It's *gut* to be here, Benjamin. Not just to help *Mamm* when she needs it, but because I needed to get away from my practice. I needed to—to de-stress, as the *Englisch* put it."

Another buggy approached, heading toward town. They both waved at the older man, who waved back. "That was Bishop Beiler," he told her.

"Samuel Beiler?"

"*Ja*."

"I remember him from when I was a *youngie*. I didn't realize he'd become the bishop."

"He's a *gut* man, fair and understanding. Everyone likes him." Benjamin grinned. "And he loves his cats."

"A man who loves animals can never be that bad." To his relief, she chuckled, seemingly over her earlier dark mood. "Oh! I forgot to tell you. Eva asked about participating in the Mountain Days demo. She said she might be interested in showcasing some baby quilts she makes."

"That's *gut*! She makes beautiful quilts. *Danke*, I've been meaning to ask her if she wanted to contribute."

"So many skills," Abigail murmured. "I have a feeling all the girls I grew up with went on to learn some amazing skills. I'm behind on so many things."

"Except a veterinarian degree," he reminded her.

"*Ja*, but that doesn't count for much when it comes time to cook dinner or sew a quilt. Although I wasn't bad at sewing," she added. "Sometimes I think I suture as well as I do because of my early training in sewing."

"We each have our own gifts."

"*Ja*, we do." Her words sounded a bit strangled.

Benjamin wondered at the reaction to what seemed like an ordinary comment, but he didn't pursue it. Something was bothering her, and it wasn't his business to probe.

Instead he reverted back to his assignment from the bishop. "I have quite a few people lined up so far for the Mountain Days festival."

He started ticking off names. "Tom Miller said he can demonstrate horseshoeing. Peter and Michael Stoltzfus will do some plowing—the *Englisch* seem especially interested in plowing with horses. I have people who said they would demonstrate leather-working, making soap and laundry detergent, and now Eva with her quilting." He rubbed his chin. "I'll admit, I've taken for granted the amazing variety of talent we have in the church. When you grow up with it, it doesn't seem like anything out of the ordinary. But I've been trying to see things in a different way—what unique demonstrations might interest the *Englisch*."

"It sounds like you've at least come to terms with the bishop's request."

"*Ja*, I suppose. I wasn't pleased at first, but I must admit the people organizing the festival have been very appreciative with what I've done so far."

He pulled up to his cabin and climbed down from the buggy. He turned to assist Abigail, but she had already gotten down.

To his surprise, she faced him and said, "Look, if you want me to help recruit some other demos for the Mountain Days festival, let me know. Alternately, since I have so much more experience with the *Englisch*, I might be able to act as a go-between. I can suggest displays that might be of interest, or something like that."

He suppressed the little frisson of pleasure her offer gave him. "*Danke!* I would appreciate that. But at the risk of looking a gift horse in the mouth, why the offer? As you've said before, you came here to help your mother."

She shrugged and looked at the bag of groceries in her hands. "*Mamm* is right. I would probably drive her nuts if I spent twenty-four hours a day with her. I don't mind having an extra project to keep busy."

"Then what I may ask you to do is keep in mind what kinds of demonstrations the women of the church can do, and I'll concentrate on the men. Would that work?"

"*Ja*, that would work. And it would give me an excuse to reacquaint myself with so many people I used to know."

"*Gut. Danke*, Abigail."

He turned to lead the horse to the barn and watched as Abigail headed back to her mother's house.

"It's a start," he murmured. And he wondered if she would ever become fully Amish.

Chapter Four

Abigail finished pinning her *kapp* over her hair and gave her mother a concerned look. "Are you sure you'll be all right by yourself?"

Esther flapped a hand. "*Ja*, sure. I don't intend to do anything except knit while you're gone. Besides, I'm getting along okay with the walker. It will be *gut* for you to attend the Sabbath service, *liebling*. So many are curious to see you again."

That was part of her reluctance to attend a Sabbath service. It's not that she was dreading it, exactly. But she knew her arrival in town had caused a buzz of speculation. About two-thirds of this new Montana Amish church was from her old hometown in Indiana, and the rest came from various other churches around the country. This meant two thirds of the people attending the service would remember her as a teenager.

So far no one had condemned her for leaving, but it certainly set her apart in a way she found uncomfortable. She realized, deep down, that she craved the good opinion of the church.

And doubtless everyone would want to know if she intended to remain—it was a question she could not yet answer.

She caught her mother's eye. With uncanny precision, Esther observed, "You're nervous about attending the service, aren't you?"

"Maybe." Abigail dropped down into a chair next to her mother. "It's been so long, *Mamm*. I don't know what everyone thinks of me. I find myself feeling defensive about the choices I've made."

"Don't borrow trouble," Esther advised. "Maybe it's because they know I'm your *mamm*, but I haven't heard anything bad about you— just wild curiosity now that you're back."

Abigail sighed. "You're right. Maybe I've built everything up in my mind to be bigger than it is. It's just that—that I've led such an unconventional life, and part of me expects to be condemned for it."

"You aren't baptized. You broke no vows or oaths," Esther said gently. "You've just been on your own journey, *liebling*. Many of us do the same thing."

"I know." Abigail toyed with the strings of her *kapp*. "And I have to stop assuming the worst. I chose to leave, and now I chose to come back for a bit. That's all."

"Remember that. Now go on, you don't want to be late."

Abigail should have known her mother would impart hardheaded common sense. *Mamm* was right—there was no reason to avoid attending a Sabbath service, which was the heart blood of the Amish community. And truth be told, she needed to be reminded of her spiritual roots that, all too often, got lost in the secular world.

"All right, I'll go," she told Esther. "But don't try anything fancy while I'm gone, *ja*?"

Esther chuckled. Abigail made sure her mother had the things she needed within easy reach. Then, taking hold of a basket of food for the after-service meal, she set out for the home of Amos and June Stoltzfus, who were hosting the week's service. Esther had told her where she would find the house.

The weather was magnificent. Ever attuned to animal life, Abigail noted white-tailed deer, turkeys—some with long-legged chicks in their wake—magpies, robins, pheasant and quail.

This land was wilder than Indiana, but the

church members were actively creating farms from the open land all around. She saw herds of dairy and beef cattle, a few places with goats or pigpens, many with hives of bees, and fields of corn and wheat. Every place had young fruit trees and flourishing gardens. Except for the towering mountains to the west, and the forests of conifers that edged them in, it looked like a typical thriving Amish community that might be found anywhere in the Midwest.

She wasn't alone in making her way toward the Stoltzfus farm. She heard the clip-clop of hooves pulling buggies. Ahead and behind her, clusters of people walked, most carrying baskets. But she walked alone…and wondered at the significance of that.

But she wasn't alone for long. As soon as she drew near the Stoltzfus farm, her friend Eva Hostetler—flanked by two young children—beckoned her over. "Abigail! Come sit with me."

"*Danke!* I will." Abigail deposited her basket of food on one of the tables set up under the shade of several magnificent fir trees. "Are these your children?"

"*Ja*, Jacob and Mildred."

"Oh, what lovely names." The children looked to be about three and five years of age. "Where is your husband? I haven't met him yet."

"He's over there. His name is Daniel."

Daniel was a pleasant-looking man, about the same height as his wife, with cheerful blue eyes over his chestnut beard. He shook her hand. "So nice to meet you. Eva has spoken of little else since bumping into you at the Yoders' store a few days ago."

"I don't remember you from our old church in Indiana," said Abigail.

"That's because I'm from Ohio," he explained. "I came to visit some family in Indiana, and that's how Eva and I met." He swung his son into his arms and planted a noisy kiss on the child's cheek. "*Komm*, I think we're seating ourselves."

Eva took her daughter by the hand and turned toward the farm's large barn, where the Sabbath service was being held. "It's so *gut* to have you back with us, Abigail."

Abigail followed Eva into the shadowy interior and found a place at a bench on the women's side.

The interior of the barn was bright and clean. "Newly built," Eva told her. "We've been having barn raisings a couple times a month since everyone is still getting their farms up and running."

"It's lovely." Abigail glanced over the benches, which were neatly set up. She nodded at Benjamin as he found a place on a bench on the men's side. "It's like our old church in Indiana was transported right here to Montana."

Eva pulled little Mildred onto her lap. "One or two families returned to Indiana because they preferred it there, but most of us like this new place. We're all starting to build up our businesses and farms. And the *Englisch* community has been wonderful."

They had no time for further chatter as Bishop Beiler stood up to announce the first hymn.

As the service progressed, Abigail realized with a sharp pang how much she missed her spiritual roots. The unity within the barn as everyone sang the familiar hymns, and then as the bishop gave his sermon, created a longing within her. She hadn't expected to be impacted so strongly by the combined kilowatts of faith.

Later, at the meal following the service, she sat among a group of women she remembered from her youth. Most of the women her age had young children and attentive husbands. Whom did she have? Nobody.

Out of the corner of her eye, she saw a black Lab belonging to the Stoltzfus children, a cheerful, healthy-looking animal…except something seemed wrong with his feet. She excused herself from the table and approached the dog, who greeted her with the enthusiasm of all Labrador retrievers.

The animal's toenails had overgrown severely, which made him walk gingerly. It was an easy fix and she had nail clippers back at the house.

"You would trim them for me?" said June Stoltzfus, when Abigail thanked her for hosting the Sabbath service and offered to treat the dog.

"*Ja*, sure. If you want to bring the dog to *Mamm*'s house anytime this week, it won't take much time to trim them. Besides, I'm sure *Mamm* would love to see you." She leaned down and tousled the dog's ears. "He seems like such a nice boy."

"Oh, he is. Our kids love him. *Ja*, I'll bring him by. Tomorrow, perhaps?"

"*Ja*, tomorrow will work fine. Afternoon would be best."

"And I'll have a chance to visit with your mother, too. *Danke*, Abigail. It's so nice to have you back."

Abigail gathered up her basket and the empty food containers, then started on the road back home.

"How was your first Sabbath service?" called a voice from behind.

Startled, she turned. Benjamin jogged to

catch up with her. She waited until he was next to her before answering. "Fine. It was nice to see everyone again. Everyone wanted to know if I'm staying."

He fell into step beside her, which created a certain intimacy. She was uneasily aware that courting couples often walked home from church together.

"So…have you made up your mind?" he asked. "About whether you're staying?"

"How can I?" She glared at him. "I've only been here a couple weeks. That's not something I can decide in such a short amount of time."

"What's holding you back?"

"A doctorate in veterinary science and two years of active practicing," she snapped.

"Don't take it out on me," he said mildly.

Her pride deflated in a heartbeat. "*Ja*, you're right. I'm sorry, Benjamin. It's a touchy subject for me. I spent years and years in school, and I finally got to achieve my dream of working with animals."

"But at what cost?"

The simple question nearly undid her. The *cost* had been readily apparent at the Sabbath service—a loving husband, a gaggle of children, a solid place within the church community. The cost, in fact, was enormous. Her eyes prickled. "Let's talk about something else."

"*Ja*, sure." Benjamin gestured around them. "Did you notice that most of the farms belonging to church members are clustered in this little valley?"

Distracted, she followed his motion. "*Nein*, not really. Why is that?"

"Because the church bought a huge ranch that was up for sale, and parceled it out to church members. The only downside is not many have homes big enough to host Sabbath services or other events, so poor Amos and June Stoltzfus end up hosting more often than they'd like, since they have a large house and barn."

"You said sometimes people meet at the Millers' building in town?"

"*Ja*, but we prefer to keep Sabbath services closer in. In many ways buying up that big ranch was an ideal arrangement—it keeps us all clustered close together, where we can help each other, and caused no hard feelings among the *Englisch* in town. I may not be fond of the *Englisch*, but I must admit we've had no problems with them."

Abigail drew her eyebrows together. "You've mentioned several times you're not fond of the *Englisch*, yet each time you also admit everyone in town has been open and welcoming. That's quite a contradiction, Benjamin. What have the *Englisch* ever done to you?"

Benjamin was momentarily broadsided by Abigail's blunt question. He didn't feel like getting into his romantic past or the issue with his older sister.

But before he could answer, a buggy came up from behind and slowed beside them. Benjamin saw the earnest face of Eva Hostetler's father, Eli Miller.

Abigail paused. "*Guder nammidaag*, Eli."

"*Guder nammidaag.* I meant to ask you something at the Sabbath service, but I forgot. I have a cow whose mastitis is worsening. Can you look at her tomorrow?"

"*Ja*, sure." He saw her frown. "Is it urgent? Should I come today?"

"*Nein*, tomorrow should be fine."

"Tell me, does she have a calf on her at all?"

"*Ja.* I only milk her once a day, in the morning. The rest of the time she has a calf on her."

Her expression cleared. "*Gut.* I think I have some cephalosporin in my kit. What time do you want me there?"

"Morning might be best."

"I'll be there."

"Vielen Dank." Eli tipped his hat, turned the buggy and headed in the other direction.

"Mastitis with a calf," she murmured.

"Is that unusual?"

"*Ja.* Mastitis most often happens when cows don't have calves on them. But the constant nursing of a calf can clear up a mild case of mastitis quickly. I'll have to see the situation when I get there tomorrow." She started walking again.

He kept pace with her. "Here's something to think about. You said you weren't interested in being hired by the local veterinarian clinic. But have you thought about opening up your own clinic just for the church community?"

She arched her eyebrows. "But I told you, I'm not licensed in Montana. That would be against the law."

"Not if you don't charge anything."

"Benjamin, what are you talking about?"

"I mean, people are already asking you for help with their animals. I know I did, when Lydia broke her leg. Opening up a temporary clinic might be a *gut* way to keep your skills fresh while caring for your *mamm*. It would also…well, it might be a shortcut way to gain respect with the church community. A way of proving you did the right thing by becoming a vet, if you will."

She lifted her chin. "I don't think I did the wrong thing by becoming a vet."

He sighed. "I didn't say you did. I'm not here to argue, Abigail. I'm just making a point."

"You're right." She let out a deep breath. "Sorry. I feel like an outsider. It's just a personal issue I have to deal with."

"We're nearly home, so look over there." He pointed. "See that small shed? I'm not using it, but it's in fairly *gut* shape. I could outfit that for you as a sort of ad hoc clinic, if you're interested. We can look at it tomorrow afternoon, if you want."

"I don't know..." she hedged. "There's only so much I can do if I don't have the proper equipment at my disposal. X-ray machine, surgical facilities..."

"Do you always underrate yourself this way?"

She snapped her mouth shut and looked a bit shell-shocked. Then she gave him a rueful smile. "I didn't used to. All right, let's look at it tomorrow."

He accompanied her to the guesthouse and followed her indoors. Esther was sitting by the open window, knitting.

"*Mamm?* How are you feeling?" Abigail placed her basket on the floor, then bent and kissed the older woman's cheek.

"*Gut.* Fairly *gut. Guder nammidaag,* Benjamin. How was the Sabbath service?"

"Excellent. Everyone asked about you." He smiled at her. "And your daughter has an appointment to see Eli Miller's cow tomorrow about a case of mastitis."

"Ain't so?" Esther turned toward Abigail. "So your concerns about people shunning you because you left aren't coming true, then?"

"It appears not." Abigail glanced at him. "Also, June Stoltzfus is coming over tomorrow so I can clip her dog's nails. They're badly overgrown. I told her you'd enjoy visiting with her."

"*Ach, ja.* June is such a nice woman."

Benjamin nodded. "Apparently I'm not the only one who needs her expertise when it comes to injuries," he said. "In fact, tomorrow we're going to look at a small outbuilding I have that might work as an ad hoc vet clinic."

"Vet clinic! But I thought—"

"I know what you thought, *Mamm,* because I thought it, too," Abigail interrupted. "I'm not licensed here, so I can't charge anything. Plus, I'm limited in what I can do because I don't have any equipment. But maybe I'm being pushed in this direction since everyone keeps asking for help with their animals."

"Perhaps *guided* is the better word," Esther

said gently. "Don't underestimate your gifts, *liebling*." She flapped a hand. "I'm fine sitting here, so why don't you go look at the shed right now? I'm curious to hear about it."

Benjamin lifted an eyebrow and glanced at her. "Will that work? We can look at it now."

She shrugged. "Sure."

"We won't be long," he told Esther.

He led the way toward a shed with a low peaked roof about twenty feet square. "There are lots of little outbuildings on this property," he explained as they approached the structure. "I actually have more than I need, so I've never used this one. But it has easy road access for buggies or wagons."

"And it has a little corral in back." Abigail approached the fence of the corral and rested her hands on the top rail. "An injured horse or cow could stay here for treatment."

"*Ja*, and I could build a small shelter right there for protection."

"You would do that?" She angled a glance in his direction.

"Let's call it a gratitude payment for setting Lydia's leg."

She bit her lip, then said, "Let's look inside."

The shed was cool and dark inside, with a wooden floor, bare stud walls and no wallboard. He looked around. "Somebody had plans for this place," he noted. "See? The walls are insulated." He pointed to the pink fiberglass batting covered with clear plastic. "And I don't see any water damage, so it looks like the roof is tight."

Abigail glanced around. "It would need a few windows for light."

"I have some old windows that were left in the barn when I bought this place. They wouldn't be hard to install."

"I can probably scrounge some furniture and tables."

"Or I could make some. I'm a carpenter, remember?"

She looked around, then crossed her arms and hugged herself. "It might work!" Her eyes sparkled in the dimness of the room.

He chuckled. "I don't think I've seen you so happy since you got here." Her whole face was lit up, as if with an inner light. "Have you missed practicing animal medicine that much?"

"It's not so much a matter of *missing* it as being *called* toward it." She scanned the small room. "Thank you, Benjamin. I don't know how much use I'll make of this as a clinic, but it will be nice to have a place set up."

"You might look through my barn at some point, too." He angled his head toward the doorway to a large older wooden barn, weathered and sturdy. "When the church bought this ranch, whoever was living here left behind many useful things I haven't needed so far. The windows, for example. I can install several in here without much problem."

"I don't want to take you away from your own work," said Abigail, frowning. "It sounds like this whole Mountain Days exhibition stuff you're doing takes a lot out of you." She fiddled with the strings of her *kapp*. "But maybe turnabout's fair play. If you help me set this place up as a clinic, I'll do what I can to help you organize the Mountain Days exhibits and demonstrations. I have more experience dealing with the *Englisch*, so it's not such an onerous task for me."

He felt simultaneously relieved and disturbed. Relieved, because it would be nice to share the burden of the project, and disturbed because it was a clear reminder that Abigail wasn't Amish.

"Ja, danke" was all he said. "Maybe you could talk to Eli Miller tomorrow when you look at his cow. He and his oldest son do leatherworking for bridles and harnesses. I've been

try to talk them into setting up an exhibit about how they work leather, but they say it's *hochmut*. Proud."

"*Ja*, sure, I'll see what I can do." Abigail met his eyes in the gloom of the building. "The *Englisch* aren't so bad, Benjamin. Don't make them into a bigger problem than they are. I met many wonderful *Englisch* during my time away, and I've come to appreciate them. Sure, there are a few bad eggs, but aren't there a few of those within our own church, too?"

"I suppose." He looked at his shoes and scuffed some dirt on the floor, then muttered, "I just wish they'd give back what they swallow sometimes."

"I came back, didn't I?"

Startled, he looked up. "But you're not back," he said flatly. "Not really. You're here to help Esther, and when she's well you'll be swallowed up again, too, just like—" He stopped.

Abigail reached out and touched his arm, then dropped her hand. "Tell me about it someday," she said quietly. "For now, I must make sure *Mamm* has everything she needs. *Danke*, Benjamin."

And she was gone. He stared after her slender figure as she picked her way across a rough patch of driveway, ever alert to the sights and sounds of nature around her.

For just a moment, he saw Barbara walking away. Then he blinked away the memory and realized Abigail—at least so far—was still here.

Chapter Five

Abigail rummaged through her trunk of veterinary supplies, pulling out everything related to mastitis in cows and packing it into a basket. "I'm going to have to order more supplies if this keeps up," she remarked to her mother. "This may look like a lot, but overall it's not much more than a first-aid kit. But I find myself looking forward to setting up a free clinic, even if I'm limited in what I can do."

Esther looked up from her seat at the table, where she was making piecrust cookies. "Just as I'm looking forward to June Stoltzfus coming over this afternoon. I know you'll be trimming her dog's nails, but it seems like ages since I had a *gut* chat with someone besides you and Benjamin."

"You're getting more mobile, so having visitors should be fine." Abigail leaned forward and kissed her mother's cheek. "I'll be back before June comes by, so don't worry about making tea. I can do it when I get back."

She picked up the basket of vet supplies and took off for the Miller farm, which Esther had told her was about a mile away. Puffy clouds piled up and it looked likely to rain later in the day, so she was glad to take care of the cow while the weather held.

Eva's parents, Eli and Anna Miller, had a lovely white clapboard house with a barn that looked newly built. Abigail recalled what Eva had said, about barn raisings taking place frequently as the church community built up their farms. She saw a large and tidy garden, a yard bordered by colorful flowers, a coop with chickens and a number of handsome Jersey cows grazing with calves alongside them. The Millers might be new to the area, but they'd gone a long way toward setting up a workable farm.

"*Guder mariye*, Abigail," greeted Anna, who came to the door with a dusting of flour on her apron. "Thank you for coming by. Eli is in the barn. *Komm*, I'll show you where."

Abigail followed Anna's plump figure through the barn door into the shadowy interior. Eli, a pitchfork in hand, was cleaning stalls.

"Guder mariye." He leaned the pitchfork against a wall and brushed off his hands. "Let me show you where the cow is."

"Is she a Jersey?" asked Abigail, picking her way amid a clutter of barnyard tools Eli evidently stored wherever he wished. "I saw other Jerseys in your pasture."

"Ja. She's four years old. This is her second calf."

"Did she have mastitis with her first calf?"

"Ja, and I treated it with intramammary infusions until it cleared up. But this time it seems more stubborn. Here she is," he added.

Abigail put her basket on the barn floor and leaned on the gate top. A buff-colored animal, her huge brown eyes gentle and patient, regarded her while chewing her cud. A calf, darker in color, was lying near its mother.

"Her eyes look good," noted Abigail. "A bad infection can often dull their eyes. Is she eating well?"

"Ja. I'm keeping her separated from the other cows. I don't want any cross contamination."

Abigail silently blessed the diligent farmer for his caution. She'd met many livestock owners who were not nearly as careful, then blamed the vet when infections spread.

She rummaged in her basket and withdrew a

thermometer and a test cup with a snap-down lid, then opened the gate and stepped inside the stall. With a heave, the cow rose to her feet. The calf scampered to a far corner and stood, watching. After petting the large animal, Abigail ran a hand over her lymph nodes. She worked her way over the cow's body until she reached the udder. She probed and squeezed, extracting milk from each quarter into the test cup. Three of the quarters were fine; the fourth quarter had the telltale squiggly indications of mastitis. But the squiggles were white and not brown, and the smell wasn't strong. The animal's temperature was a bit elevated, but not badly so.

"She's in fairly *gut* shape," she told Eli. "The mastitis might be persistent, but it's not a bad infection. She'll need monitoring. Keep the calf with her at all times—don't separate them at night—and let's see how she does. I have some antibiotics, but I'd rather not use them if possible. Better to let nature heal her. But if you notice a change for the worse, let me know immediately and we'll take a more aggressive approach." Abigail scratched the animal on her forehead. "She's a sweet girl. I can see why you're fond of her."

"*Ja*, I am. Up until this point, she's been my best milker, too."

"We'll see if we can return her to that state." Abigail wiped down the thermometer and snapped the lid on the test cup. She didn't want to risk infected milk spilling anywhere. "I understand you own the building in town that takes in lodgers. Do you run it as a motel?"

Eli rubbed his chin. "Not quite. It's become more of a meeting hall and a place for church members to stay when they visit from out of town. But we've taken *Englisch* guests, too. I guess you could say it's more like a bed-and-breakfast. Our middle son, Matthew, is doing the day-to-day operations. He says it keeps him from milking cows, so he's happy." His eyes twinkled.

Abigail chuckled. "But you won't give up your cows?"

"*Nein.* I love them too much." He slapped the bovine affectionately on the flank.

Abigail repacked her vet supplies into the basket. Then, remembering her promise to Benjamin, she said, "And you're a leather worker, *ja*?"

"That's right. My oldest son and I make harnesses and bridles." Eli pointed to the halter on the cow's head. "Halters, too. That's one of the ones we made."

Abigail examined the halter, which was

well-made and fit the cow perfectly. "Where do you get your leather?"

"I get donated hides and we work it ourselves."

Surprised, Abigail turned to him. "You work the leather from start to finish? You don't purchase your leather already cured?"

"*Nein*, I like to work it a certain way for harnesses and reins, and I can't purchase the quality of leather I prefer. Or perhaps I should say, the quality of leather I prefer is too expensive. Better to work it myself." He gave a rueful smile.

"Have you thought about showing your technique at the Mountain Days demonstration?"

Eli frowned. "Benjamin already talked to me about that. I don't think so. That would be *hochmut*. Proud. And the *Englisch* would likely have cameras."

"I wonder," mused Abigail, "if Benjamin could put up a sign for no photography? I think it would be easier for many church members to participate if they knew cameras weren't permitted."

"He could put up a sign, but I don't know if it will do any *gut*," said Eli. "Taking pictures seems to be too popular to stop by putting up a sign."

"*Ja.*" Abigail rubbed her chin and decided

on a little honesty. "But, Eli, I think Benjamin is trying his best to do what the bishop asked. He didn't especially want this assignment to work on the Mountain Days demo, but the bishop wanted him to showcase as many skills as possible from the church community. I think he would consider it a personal favor if you were to do some sort of leather demonstration."

Eli looked a bit guilt-stricken. "I didn't think of that. *Ja*, I'd forgotten the bishop asked Benjamin to organize this." He sighed. "I suppose my son and I can pull something together."

Abigail kept her face serious, but inside she was smiling. "I'm certain both Benjamin and Bishop Beiler would be grateful," she told him.

"And Anna, she makes soft candies," Eli volunteered unexpectedly. "I suppose she could put together a demonstration on that. We have a propane burner for heating the sugar."

"*Danke!* I'm sure that would be welcome." Abigail thought it best to beat a hasty retreat before Eli changed his mind. She gave the cow a gentle slap on the back. "Keep me posted about this lady, but something tells me she'll be fine. I'll come back in a week to check her out."

"*Vielen Dank.*" He opened the pen gate for

her. "Are you planning on opening up a clinic while you're here?"

"Funny you should ask," she replied. "I can't legally work here in Montana because I'm only licensed in Indiana, but I don't mind doing some unpaid things here and there. I might be setting up a temporary clinic in a small building near *Mamm*'s house. I can't do anything complicated because I don't have much equipment, but I suppose I can do some things. However, I can't be paid."

"Then consider the leather demonstration as payment." Eli smiled.

Abigail grinned. "*Danke!* That's more than enough. Benjamin has been very *gut* to my mother, so I've been helping him out on this project."

She took her basket and walked back down the road, enjoying the scenery, sniffing the fresh mountain air, listening to the birdsong. She liked this little corner of Montana. Above all, it was good to be out of the busy Indianapolis clinic where she'd been practicing and back among farms.

And the church community. A place where she understood the people, and they understood her.

Her mother was improving. Soon Esther wouldn't need any help around the household at all, certainly within the two months Abigail was supposed to stay here. What then? How long could she use her mother's health to avoid thinking about her own future?

She frowned. She hadn't been fired after her tiff with Robert, so in theory she could return to the Indiana clinic and continue doing what she did best: caring for animals. But feminine instinct told her she would never again be comfortable working for him—not just because of his volatile temper, but also because her own emotions had been too tied up with her work situation.

Her mind turned toward the vet clinic in the town of Pierce. She hadn't yet gone in to talk with anyone, but she wondered if they were hiring. Then again, did she want to be so close to the church community but not be a baptized member? She wasn't certain baptism would be permitted for someone in her position—a working professional.

Maybe it was time to talk to the bishop.

"You did what?" Benjamin stared at Abigail as she placed a lunch basket on his workbench and bent down to pet Lydia, whose tail swished in welcome.

She smiled. "I talked Eli and Anna Miller both into participating in the Mountain Days demos. Eli will demonstrate how he works leather, and Anna will be making some soft candies."

He dropped onto a stool and stared at her. "I've been after Eli for a month now, but he's refused to participate. He's been a tough nut to crack. How did you do it?"

"I think part of it was as a sort of payment for looking at his cow this morning. But his biggest concerns were *hochmut* and photography. I reminded him it was the bishop who asked you to arrange these demonstrations, so participating wouldn't be a matter of *hochmut*. And I suggested you might put up prominent signage—for all the good it may do—asking people to refrain from taking photos."

"*Ja, gut,* I can do that." He looked at her with admiration. She had an impish sparkle in her eyes and he could tell she was pleased by her morning's work. He rubbed his chin. "Since you've gotten here, three new people have agreed to do demonstrations—both the Millers, and Eva Hostetler as well. And all thanks to you."

"Well, it's just one family, when you think about it."

"But still." He smiled. "This project might turn out better than I'd hoped. I'm beginning to sense a bit of enthusiasm from people."

"And from you, too."

"Me?"

"*Ja*, you." Abigail opened the lunch basket and took out some containers, which she set out for him. "Your attitude appears to be changing. When you first mentioned this assignment from the bishop, quite honestly you weren't happy about it. Now you seem different."

"Hmm." It pained him to admit she might be right. "As I said, I'm hoping it will revitalize my business."

"Or maybe it's because you have a penchant for organization," she replied. "You said you thought the bishop chose you to organize these demonstrations because you were unmarried and had more time, but I wonder if he didn't ask you because you have a talent you didn't know you had?" She smiled. "See you at dinner." After placing the basket on the floor, she gave the dog one last pat, then walked out the shop door.

He stared after her. Could she be right? Did he have a penchant for organization? Could he have invented his resentment toward this assignment from the bishop as a means to overcome his aversion to the *Englisch*, when in fact the bishop simply recognized a talent instead? It was something to mull over.

He ate lunch, then set aside the empty containers and resumed his work building kitchen seating for the large Graber family, who had requested a dozen chairs. He methodically slotted the wood and inserted pegs to join the pieces for the chair frames while thinking about the fascinating woman who'd entered his life. If he wasn't careful, he could let Abigail occupy a good portion of his thoughts. If only...

If only Abigail hadn't followed the same path as the woman he'd courted so long ago, lured into the wider world by the glittering possibilities it offered. Glitter. That was the word he used to describe it. The glitter of a career, the glitter of fashion, the glitter of automobiles and cell phones and movies and all the things he shunned. Barbara had succumbed to that glitter, and that's the only reason he could think Abigail had left the church as well—the allure of a career as a veterinarian.

Could he persuade her to stay? Could a quiet life outside of a small town in Montana compete with the glitter of her work in Indiana? Did he dare risk his heart with a woman for whom the glittering *Englisch* world was an attraction?

He stood back and looked at his handiwork. Twelve partially finished chair frames leaned against the wall, pegged with oak and strengthened with wood glue. He couldn't do much more until the glue dried. He looked at the empty food containers Abigail had left for his lunch, and decided to return them. He could talk with her about plans for the ad hoc clinic. Deep down he knew it was just an excuse to see her.

He placed the empty containers in the basket, pocketed a tape measure and small notepad, and started down the path toward Esther's cottage.

From a distance, he saw Abigail sitting on the front porch, her back against a post and one leg dangling off the edge. Something was with her. Curious, he slipped behind a tree and peered around for a closer look.

A handsome black dog, a Labrador, was lying beside her with his head in her lap. She absently stroked the animal's fur while gazing out at the scenery.

For some reason he felt his throat close up. He was spying on her during a private moment, but her pose epitomized so much about this woman. The dog's trusting position, with his head in her lap, demonstrated Abigail's absolute affinity for animals.

She didn't look like the type to be pulled

away by the glittering outside world, but what other explanation was there?

He squared his shoulders and continued down the drive, his feet crunching on the gravel. Both Abigail and the dog turned to watch him approach.

"I thought I'd bring the basket back early," he said. "I have some chairs half-finished in the shop and can't do anything more until they're dry."

"I see." The dog dropped his head back in her lap, watching him with alert chocolate-brown eyes.

"Who's this guy?" Benjamin bent down to pet the dog before sitting on the porch as well.

"He belongs to Amos and June Stoltzfus. June brought him over so I could trim his nails, and stayed to visit with *Mamm*."

Through the open window, he could hear the murmur of feminine voices and the clink of tea things. "I'm glad Esther has a visitor. I imagine she was getting a bit lonely."

"I thought so, too." She stroked the dog's fur. "That's why I invited June over. I thought it best to stay out of their way and let them visit."

"Then we have a chance to discuss your clinic." He gestured toward the outbuilding a short distance away. "I brought a tape measure and notepad, so we can talk about specifics."

"*Ja!* I'd like that."

"I can start putting a little time into it each afternoon to retrofit it," he offered. "I'll start with windows, since those will need to be done first. I also have a roll of linoleum that was left in my barn. I can use that for the flooring if you want—it will be waterproof."

"I can't believe you're willing to do all this work for me."

He was silent a moment. "I've got time," he admitted. "My business is slow at the moment. I don't have enough orders to fill my day. Besides, I can't tell you how grateful I am you helped Lydia. She's my favorite dog."

"Glad to help. How long before her puppies are due?"

"A couple weeks."

"Come and get me when she goes into labor. I want to be there just in case."

"So…do you want to walk over and look at the clinic building?"

"Sure." She rose and dusted off the back of her dress, then stepped toward the open window. "*Mamm?* I'm walking over to look at that outbuilding with Benjamin. June, I'll take the dog with me. He'll enjoy the walk."

"*Ja, danke,*" June replied from inside.

"So I wonder," Abigail remarked as they stepped off the porch, followed by the eager dog, "what are June's skills that could be demonstrated?"

"You mean, for the Mountain Days event?"

"*Ja*, what else?"

"Hmm." He stroked his chin. "She makes the best pies in the church. She sells them in the Yoders' store. But it's not like she can put on a pie-making demo."

"Why not? If her pies sell, it's because people may prefer to buy them ready-made than make their own. Maybe she could put up a demo showing why her pies are especially *gut*."

He chuckled, then stopped when he realized she was serious. "Do you think she would agree?"

"All you can do is ask." She smiled.

"Abigail, you're amazing." He grinned back. "At this rate, the whole church community will be participating."

"That's what you want, isn't it? Or at least, what the bishop wants."

"*Ja.*" He was silent a moment, envisioning the variety of booths that might be set up in the demonstration area. In his mind's eye, he could see colorful bunting, clear signage and interested visitors. "It will be *gut*," he murmured to himself.

"What, the demo?"

"*Ja.* I'm just envisioning how it would look."

"I'm thinking it will turn out much better than you might think. Come on, Benjamin. Do you really think anyone who agreed to participate will let you down? And once this demo is over, maybe you won't be so hostile to *me*."

He nearly staggered backward. "Hostile toward *you*? Have I shown myself to be hostile toward you?"

She shrugged. "Maybe not me personally, but I'm a lot more *Englisch* than you like, and you don't like the *Englisch*." She glanced at him, then looked at the ground.

"Glitter," he muttered.

"What?"

"Nothing."

She crossed her arms. "Would you care to explain yourself? Because you're being hostile again."

He felt a shaft of anger. "Deal with it."

"Fine." She turned and started to stomp away.

Benjamin's anger turned to shame. "Abigail, wait."

She stopped but kept her rigid back toward him. The silence lengthened. Finally she said, "Well?"

"Look, I'm wary of the *Englisch* world for reasons of my own, There's just too much glitter out there. It pulls people away from the community."

She looked at him. "What do you mean by glitter?"

"Attractions. Excitement. Change. Cars, electronics, movies, fashion, jewelry, shopping. All the things we shun. It entices those who might already have a rebellious streak, those with a determination to see the wider world. I know now we shun those things for *gut* reason. They pull people away. You're no different," he added, then immediately wanted to snatch back the words.

The utter shock on her face made him sorry he'd brought up the whole matter, but now there was no going back.

"Is that what you think?" she finally choked out. "Do you honestly think it was 'glitter' that took me away from my family and my church when I was eighteen?"

"Wasn't it?"

"Nein!" She glared at him. "I've come to admire many things in the *Englisch* world, but leaving the Amish had nothing to do with all that. I left to go to school and become a vet!"

"Hochmut," he muttered.

She poked an index finger against his chest. "Don't accuse me of *hochmut* without evidence, Benjamin."

"But that's part of why you succeeded, isn't it? *Hochmut?*"

"Wrong again." She shook her head and leaned against a fence rail. "You're making a lot of assumptions."

"Then why did you leave? What caused you to want to be a vet if it wasn't *hochmut* or the attractions of the *Englisch* world?"

"It was *Gott.*" She lifted her chin.

He stared. "*Gott* told you to leave our church?"

"In a manner of speaking." She sighed. "Let me explain."

Chapter Six

Abigail dropped down to sit on a long length of log near the fence. The black Lab selected a stick and lay down to gnaw it. "Did *Mamm* ever tell you anything about how much I loved animals as a child?"

Benjamin straddled the log and picked at some bark. "A bit, but everyone knew it. You were always doing something with dogs, or cows, or cats. Didn't you once fix a bird's broken wing?"

"*Ja*. I'm surprised you remember that. But I think it stems from when I was seven or eight years old. One of my favorite cows was sick, and a veterinarian came out to look at her. Next thing I remember, the cow was fine. It was an amazing moment for me, realizing that a person could cure an animal. From that moment on, I knew I wanted to do the same thing. Not because of *hochmut*, but because *Gott* called me to be a vet."

"How can you be so sure it was *Gott*?" He looked skeptical.

"Because I've prayed on it. I spent years praying on it. It wasn't a whimsical decision or a rebellious phase. *Gott* gave me my affinity for animals from when I was a child, and medicine is the best use of that gift. Vet school was tough, but I always felt I had a higher purpose. A calling. A gift."

He shook his head. "I find that hard to believe."

"Have you never had a calling, Benjamin?" She met his eyes. "It's a powerful thing, sometimes a frightening thing. It's a gift, yes—but it can also be a torment. To follow my calling, I had to leave my family and my church. That wasn't easy to do at eighteen. But if I hadn't left, I would have felt I wasn't doing what *Gott* directed me to do."

"Are you glad you left?"

"Ja. Nein." She looked at the ground. "It's complicated. I'm glad to have developed the skills, but I've given up so much..." She trailed off.

"Ja, you're alone," he said bluntly. "You have no *hutband*, no children. For an Amish woman, those are serious sacrifices."

She turned away and focused on the mountains to the west. He was right. She had denied those yearnings for many years, which was easy in the *Englisch* world, with its emphasis on career. But would that denial haunt her as she grew older?

"I had no choice," she said softly. "It's what *Gott* wanted me to do."

"Is that a decision you'll be happy with ten years from now? Twenty years? Thirty years?"

"How could I turn down my gift?" She felt a flare of anger inside her and strove to keep her voice from reflecting it. "It's all over the Scriptures that we have different gifts from *Gott*, and we have to use those gifts to His glory. How can I throw my gift back in His face?"

"So you're staying if you stopped being a veterinarian to raise a family, that would be a decision you'd regret," stated Benjamin.

"Maybe." She noted a bald eagle sitting on a distant tree, and kept her gaze focused on the magnificent bird. "*Ja*, I'm sure of it. In a way, that's why it's such an adjustment to be back in the church community. Here, career is subsumed by faith and cooperation. I've missed that. But am I willing to sacrifice what I've worked ten years to achieve? Being a vet is not just a career, not just a job. It's *Gott*'s gift to me, and I can't push it aside."

"Let me ask you something." Benjamin continued to pick at the bark on the log. "Let's say for the sake of argument you could practice being a vet here, as an Amish woman. Would you want to?"

"*Ja*, sure, of course. But I can't. It's not acceptable. Amish women are encouraged to put family first, and if I was a practicing veterinarian, that wouldn't be possible."

"With *Gott*, all things are possible," he intoned. "But I think you're being a little too rigid. You're making assumptions that may not apply. Maybe you should talk to the bishop to see what your options are."

She felt a gleam of wry humor. "I've avoided the bishop since arriving here in town. I know precisely what he would say, and maybe I just don't want to hear it in person."

"You're going to have to talk to him at some point, anyway," he warned.

"Not if I leave again." She saw his face shutter.

"And is that what you want?"

"Benjamin, you know I'm not here for the long term. I'm just here to heal…" Her voice trailed off. She hadn't meant to say that.

Sure enough, he looked at her sharply. "Heal? Heal what?"

"Nothing."

"Abigail, lying is a sin. You know that." She heard a faint note of teasing in his voice.

She felt pressure build up inside, a need to confess. She sighed and reached down to pet the comforting dog at her feet. "Did *Mamm* tell you why I came home?"

"Your *mamm* doesn't gossip, so all I know is you came home to take care of her after her hip surgery."

"Let's just say the timing was perfect." Her voice cracked. "I messed up, Benjamin. I made a professional mistake in the clinic in which I worked, and a beautiful dog nearly died as a result. My boss—his name is Robert—was able to save him, and he dressed me down for my incompetence. As a result, I got to where I lacked confidence in my own skills. I had to leave for a while. Let's call it a leave of absence." Embarrassed, she felt herself blush. She didn't want Benjamin to know she had fancied herself in love with Robert.

To her annoyance, Benjamin stated the obvious. "You're blushing. Was that *all* that happened?"

She felt her blush deepen. "*Ja*, that's all," she snapped.

"Why do I think you're lying again? Or at least omitting something?"

"It's none of your business, Benjamin."

"As you say." He quirked a smile at her. "Though it occurs to me there might be a man involved."

She glared, then abruptly laughed. "You're incorrigible. Okay, if you want the truth, I fancied myself in love with Robert. I created a whole scenario in my mind of us marrying. It seemed so right—two professionals sharing a mutual love of animal medicine. Then when he yelled at me after nearly losing the dog, my little fantasy went right down the drain. It's like the blinders were stripped off my eyes and I saw him for what he was truly like—a man with a volatile temper who would have made a terrible *hutband*. And don't you *dare* tell *Mamm* I said that," she added fiercely.

"I wouldn't dream of it." His tone was definitely teasing. "Did this Robert ever court you or indicate he was romantically interested in you?"

"*Nein*, not at all. I was painting romantic scenarios about a man who was really, at the heart of it, very professional. There was no harassment or inappropriate behavior at all. He just had a nasty temper, something most of us in the office were willing to put up with because he paid well and we knew he was a brilliant veterinarian."

"But what happens now? Is your job still open?"

"*Ja*. I took a two-month leave of absence to care for *Mamm* just about the time they hired a junior vet fresh out of school. The clinic is growing. But they want someone with more experience and told me my job will be waiting for me when I go back."

"And *are* you going back?"

She sighed, gazing at the mountains. "I don't know. I mean, I *do* know. Yes, I'll be going back…but I'll have mixed feelings about it. Here, it's easy to immerse myself back in the church community, and it's like going from one extreme to another. I turned my back on the church when I left. I didn't leave my faith behind, but I left my culture behind. I had to learn how to live like the *Englisch*, and I came to appreciate all the opportunities I had and the things I saw. It's magnetic, really. But now that I'm back…" She paused.

"Now that you're back…?" he prompted.

"I miss it." She blurted the words. "I've missed the Sabbath services. I've missed *Mamm*. I've missed the camaraderie and sense of community, the cooperation and lack of competitiveness. There's so much I've missed out on."

"Including a *hutband* and children."

"*Ja*. Seeing Eva Hostetler was an eye-opener. She's so happy. Am I happy? I don't know. That's why I'm so confused. The tug of practicing my profession is still strong. But so is the tug of the community." She peeled a piece of bark off the log and chucked it into the grasses in a petulant gesture.

Thoughts of Robert had receded in her mind since returning to the church community and reacquainting herself with some of the people she grew up with. Attending the Sabbath services was a reminder of how much she had sacrificed in her quest to develop her gift.

A thought flickered through her consciousness… Could some of the reason Robert had receded from her mind have to do with the man now sitting opposite her on a log at the edge of a Montana forest?

Benjamin was glad to hear Abigail wasn't stuck on some *Englisch* man. It didn't seem likely any romantic interests might pull her away, even though she still faced professional conflicts. He sat quietly, momentarily lost in thought.

"Now what about you?" she asked. "There's something I want to know."

"*Ja*, sure," he said absently. "What?"

"Why you're so hostile to the *Englisch*."

He snapped out of his reverie. "I'm not—"

"Benjamin, lying is a sin." She smiled as she parroted his words back to him. "You know that. And just because I bared my heart to you doesn't mean you're obligated to return the sentiment." Her words dripped sarcasm.

"Ach." He took her rebuke in the spirit it was intended and gave her a wry smile. "Okay, I'll tell you. Do you remember my sister Miriam?"

"Ja. She's your oldest sister, isn't she?"

"Middle sister. She's two years older than me, and we were always close. She wanted to become a nurse, but to do that she had to leave the church community. My parents weren't happy with her decision, of course, but they understood she had a calling from *Gott,* so they were supportive. I was less understanding. I argued with her. I said she should stay and be baptized. I was probably obnoxious about it in the way teenage boys can be obnoxious. But in the end she left and became a nurse."

"How old were you when she left?"

"Sixteen. I took it pretty hard. For a time, I didn't have anything *gut* to say about the *Englisch,* I can tell you that. It got to the point where our old bishop in Indiana had to call me in to chastise me for my attitude. I stopped badmouthing people after that, but inside, it festered."

"Oh, Benjamin…" She gave him a sympathetic look.

He continued. "I couldn't forgive. I felt hatred for the first time in my life, and it hurt. None of these feelings were directed at my sister—I love her too much for that—but I blamed the *Englisch*, unfairly and unreasonably. I've always wondered if my attitude pushed my sister away, and deep down I blamed myself. Did I not argue enough? Did I argue too much? Was my adolescent snarkiness the final spur behind her decision to leave? And then…" He lifted his gaze toward a distant horizon and bitter memories rose.

The silence lengthened. "And then…?" Abigail prompted.

"It wasn't just my sister," he said, gritting out the words. "Do you remember Barbara Eicher? We were courting about the time you left the church community and went to college."

"*Ja*, I remember her. Nice young woman. I've always wondered why you didn't marry her."

"I wanted to. Dear *Gott*, I wanted to. But she was restless. She wanted to see the *Englisch* world during her *rumspringa*. I didn't want her to go. All I could see was the same thing happening all over again as what happened to my sister—I would lose someone I loved to the *Englisch*. But this time it was the woman I wanted to marry."

"And so she left." It was a statement, not a question.

"*Ja*, she left. She moved to the city, got a job, made friends. She ended up marrying an *Englisch* man. As far as I know she's happy, but I don't stay in touch with her so I don't know for certain." A hard look crept into his eyes. "The bottom line is, I've lost two people I love to the *Englisch* world. So I question my own temperament and my ability to chase people away."

"Is that what you think?" She stared at him. "That you chased away your sister and Barbara?"

"*Ja*. It's what I think. Maybe it's not true, but sometimes even things that aren't true take hold inside, and are hard to shake off."

Like Barbara and Miriam, Abigail hadn't been baptized. Nothing was keeping her here. Her mother would heal from her surgery and not need Abigail's care any longer. Abigail's bruised heart would heal and she would head back to her clinic in Indianapolis. In short, she was transient.

But, he realized with a sinking heart, he wanted her to stay. But what could he possibly offer that could compete with the gift from *Gott* she so desired?

"Well." He tried his best to keep his voice brisk, but it came out choked. "Let's go look at the inside of the shed again and see where you want those windows."

Abigail got to her feet and dusted off her skirt. The dog also rose to his feet, then shook and wagged his tail.

"He seems much happier without those overgrown nails," she commented, patting the animal. Then she gestured. "Lead the way."

Benjamin walked around the small building with her while she pointed out the ideal placement for windows to lighten the interior and make it workable. He took measurements and marked figures in the notepad, while the dog patiently followed on their heels. He estimated the amount of time it might take to fix up the building during his off time, while in the back of his mind he wondered if she even would be around long enough to use it.

Evidently the same thought occurred to her, too. After looking over the building one last time, Abigail stepped outside, then stopped and looked at him. "Is it worth it, do you suppose?" She waved a hand at the small building. "I might leave before it gets much use."

"I don't mind." He slipped the notebook into

his pocket. "This building needs work before it can be used for anything, whether it's an ad hoc vet clinic for you or something farm-related for me."

"I don't want to take advantage of you." She bit her lip. "You've done enough, including helping *Mamm* after she moved out here—"

She broke off as June Stoltzfus came running over to them. The black Labrador ran to her side, wagging furiously. June stopped, panting, and petted the dog. "Abigail, one of the bishop's grandsons just stopped by. He said Bishop Beiler wants to know if you're available for a meeting with him."

Benjamin saw her go pale. "He wants to meet with me? Now?"

"*Ja.* I don't think it's an emergency, but I thought you should know right away."

"*Danke*, June. I'll go see him. Is his grandson still here?"

"*Nein*, he went home. *Vielen Dank* for taking care of this old boy." She tousled the dog's ears.

"It was nothing." Abigail stood rooted to the spot, watching June and the dog retreat.

"Are you okay?" He touched her arm. Two bright colors burned in her cheeks.

"Why would the bishop want to see me?"

"You've been here a couple weeks now. It's

normal for the bishop to keep track of what's going on in the church community."

To his surprise, he saw tears well up in her eyes. "Have I done something wrong? Have I offended anyone?" Her lip trembled.

"Of course not. What makes you think that?" He kept his voice firm to hearten her. "You've done nothing wrong. And remember, you're not a baptized member of the church. At the moment, that might be to your advantage."

She took a deep hiccuping breath and pressed a hand to her midsection. "I don't want to be sent away, at least until I'm ready."

"Is that what you think? That he would send you away?"

"Wouldn't you think the same thing in my position?"

"*Ja*, maybe I would," he conceded. "But you're here to take care of your *mamm*. He can hardly chastise you for that."

"When I left, Jeremy Kemp was still the bishop," she said. "What is Bishop Beiler like? Is he fair? Harsh? Stern? Kind?"

"All of the above. He does what is necessary. I've seen him harsh, and I've seen him kind. Stop panicking, Abigail. You're imagining the worst."

"*Ja*, I suppose you're right. It's a bad habit of mine."

But she didn't look convinced. Instead she seemed small and vulnerable. All of a sudden, he felt protective. "Would it help if I walked you to his house?"

She glanced at him. "It might," she admitted.

"Then let's go. No time like the present."

"Let me go tell *Mamm* first."

"Ja, gut."

He walked with her back to Esther's cabin, feeling rather than seeing the nervousness that emanated from her. But she said nothing. He rather admired her stoicism.

She climbed the porch steps and opened the door. He stayed on the porch, but heard every word through the open window.

"Mamm? Did June tell you what the bishop's grandson said?"

"Ja, liebling." Esther's voice held a trace of worry. "Are you going to see him now?"

"Ja. Benjamin said he would go with me for support."

"He's a *gut* man."

"Is there anything you need before I go?"

"Nein. Go on, *liebling.* Get it over with."

Benjamin heard her draw in a breath. *"Ja,* you're right. I won't be long… I hope."

In a few moments, she reemerged on the porch. He noticed she'd dampened back a strand or two of hair under her *kapp* and changed into a clean apron. He saw her draw back her shoulders and lift her chin. "I'm ready."

Chapter Seven

Abigail kept telling herself she shouldn't be nervous to meet with the bishop. After all, what could he do? Benjamin was right—the fact that she was not a baptized member of the church was an advantage at the moment. It's not like she could be shunned.

But her palms were sweaty and her heart was racing as if she was in trouble.

"Take it easy." Benjamin, padding along at her side, touched her icy hand. "I can tell you're still imagining the worst."

"Ja." She took a deep breath and pressed a hand to her chest. "I am, and that's *schtupid.* How much further to the bishop's house?"

"Another quarter mile, perhaps. He and his wife live in a small home near their youngest son's house."

"They're not in a *daadi haus*?"

"*Nein*. Their son didn't move here until later, so we all got together and renovated an existing building." He pointed. "There, you can just see it through those trees."

Abigail peered and saw what looked like a made-over barn perched on a wide lawn amid the pines and firs. "It doesn't look Amish," she observed.

"It's not. When the church purchased the ranch property and then parceled out the land among those of us who moved here, Lois—that's the bishop's wife—fancied this older building and said it could be fixed up. We had the work party last year."

"When is the next work party? Eva said they're being held about once a month."

"*Ja*, the next one is a couple weeks from now, over at the Herschbergers' place."

The chatter about renovations and work parties distracted her from her nervousness, and by the time they walked up the long gravel driveway to the bishop's home, she felt more composed.

"I'll wait here." Benjamin pointed to a set of chairs under the shade of a red fir.

"*Danke*, Benjamin." Abigail inhaled, squared her shoulders, walked up to the door of the home and knocked.

The bishop's wife, Lois, answered. "*Guder*

nammidaag, Abigail. Thank you for coming so quickly. My *hutband* is in his study, if you'll follow me."

Abigail followed the older woman's taller form through a comfortable living room into a small office with a window overlooking a large vegetable garden. The bishop was sitting at a desk, writing something. He stood up when she entered.

"Guder nammidaag." He reached over to shake her hand, and his eyes crinkled as he smiled. "We've never had a chance to formally meet as adults. You were still a *youngie* when you left the church, and I was not yet a bishop." He gestured toward a chair.

Abigail seated herself and relaxed at the bishop's friendly mien. "I was a little surprised to get your request…" she began, but was startled when a cat suddenly jumped in her lap.

The bishop chuckled. "I'm sorry, this lady thinks she owns the place. Meet Thomasina."

"She's beautiful." The long-haired animal had calico fur, deep green eyes and a loud purr that rumbled around the room. Abigail stroked and scratched the feline, and was rewarded when the cat literally reached up and put her paws around her neck as if hugging her. Her heart melted and she snuggled the animal.

"You can see why she's my favorite pet," the

bishop said, smiling. "She loves people and is very affectionate."

"How old is she?"

"Just two, so we have many happy years with her. Lois and I got her just after we moved here, and she's a blessing. The grandkids think the world of her, and they spoil her rotten."

"I can understand why." The cat loosened her embrace and settled on Abigail's lap, apparently content to remain there while she tickled under the animal's chin.

"Now." The bishop's face grew more grave. "You've been here helping Esther for a couple weeks, I understand. Is she improving?"

"*Ja*, quite fast. She's mobile with her walker and is eager to do more than she should. I have to hold her back from overdoing things."

He nodded. "She's a fighter, your mother. Lois took care of her immediately after her surgery."

"*Ja*, that's what *Mamm* said," Abigail acknowledged. "I've been meaning to thank her."

"Lois and Esther have been friends for years, so Lois was glad to step in. But I'm sure having you home helped Esther just as much. She missed you during the years you were gone."

"I've missed her, too." Abigail felt her eyes prickle. "*Daed* passed away while I was still in school, and I've always felt guilty I wasn't with him during his last hours. It's *gut* to be with my mother again, even for a short time."

"Which leads me to why I asked you to visit today. I've heard rumors that you're planning on opening a veterinarian clinic."

She frowned. "Just to be clear, I'm not licensed in the state of Montana, so I can't legally practice here. Benjamin has offered to retrofit a small building on his property as a clinic, but it can only be a sort of triage place. I don't have the equipment to make it a proper clinic. Nor can I charge anything for my services." She stroked the cat on her lap. "I do it for the love of animals. I'm happy to help with anything I can do, but I'll have to refer more serious cases to the clinic in town."

"I see…"

Her frown deepened. "As a matter of interest, why do you ask?"

"Do you intend to remain with us?" His words were direct.

"I—I don't know. My original goal was to stay just long enough to help *Mamm* recover. But again, why do you ask?"

"Because being a veterinarian is not the normal path for an Amish woman."

"Believe me, Bishop Beiler, no one knows that more than me. I'm simply here for a short time to recover from—from some blows in the secular world, as well as to help *Mamm* recuperate. In the meantime, if I can use my gifts to help heal any animals that are brought to me, I see no harm in that."

"And that's what I'm leading to." He leaned back in his chair and steepled his fingers. "I'm concerned about the example you're giving to the church's young people. As you know all too well, the *Ordnung* discourages worldly pursuits. A professional degree—no matter how useful—is seen as prideful. If you remain with us, you would have to sacrifice your career to be baptized. If you plan to open a clinic, you're welcome to do so, but you will have to forgo becoming fully Amish."

Abigail felt a flush of anger. "So those are my choices," she stated through clenched teeth.

"*Ja*, those are your choices."

Fresh on the heels of her earlier conversation with Benjamin, Abigail felt more defensive than she might otherwise be. "Bishop Beiler, I became a veterinarian because of a calling from *Gott*, just as you followed *Gott*'s call to become the bishop. Could *you* so easily have refused His calling?"

His face hardened. "You know I couldn't. But that's hardly the same thing."

"It's *exactly* the same thing. A gift is a gift. Benjamin tells me you've been an outstanding bishop, so you've used your calling to serve others. My calling is animal medicine, which I feel I am also using to serve others."

"I understand that. But I'm concerned that you might be setting a bad example. Your education and success as a veterinarian might unintentionally encourage other young people to leave the community to follow a path into the *Englisch* world."

"You know I would never encourage anyone to do that."

"Perhaps not on purpose, but your very presence may act as an encouragement."

"How?" Her temper threatened to bubble over, and she clamped it down. "I've hardly even seen any *youngies* since I got here. Most of my time has been spent with *Mamm*."

"Everyone, including the *youngies* who were toddlers when you left, knows what path you took. That's why there's been such a buzz of interest when you returned to our community. I've overheard conversation among *youngies* expressing admiration for what you did. That concerns me."

"I know I followed an unusual path, but what would you have had me do? Refuse my calling?"

"Not at all. You're not baptized. You were free to do whatever you wished. But you have to understand there would be repercussions within the church family as a result."

"Meaning, I'm not welcome here." She glared.

"I didn't say that." The bishop's voice was patient. "But you chose a different path, one that took you away from the community. It's not reasonable to expect no fallout from that decision. This is the point I want to emphasize to the *youngies*."

"You're assuming everyone is eager to leave the church," she argued, "but that's not the case. Everyone's paths in life are different. So are their journeys with *Gott*."

"Abigail, I'll be blunt. I have my reservations about your return." He frowned.

She felt her face flush with anger. "Since you're being blunt, then tell me what you want me to do. Do you want me to leave?"

"*Nein...*"

"*Gut*, because I'm here to take care of *Mamm* after her surgery, and I won't leave until she's better. *Mamm* is improving. Probably within four or five weeks, she won't need me any longer. Then I can turn my back on this community and you won't have to see me anymore." She scooped up the cat, placed it on his desk and stumbled out of the room.

She went outside, blinded by tears. Benjamin scrambled to her side as she began walking. She was thankful he didn't pepper her with questions, but merely handed her a folded handkerchief. She nodded and buried her face in it. Her shoulders heaved.

How dare the bishop question her gift? How dare he give her an ultimatum?

She didn't like how glibly he dismissed her calling as trivial and unimportant, as if the difficult decision to leave and train herself in the veterinary sciences was a childish whim or girlish impulse. She had answered a call, just as the bishop himself had, to serve *Gott* as best she could. Why could he not understand that?

Deep down she knew his lecture was inevitable. The choice she had been avoiding was now upon her. She had to make a decision whether she wanted to stay, give up her career and join the church community of her birth. Or if she would leave, and abandon the faith and way of life in what she now realized had been an anchor for her.

Always in the back of her mind, during all the years of her schooling and practice, she knew she wanted the opportunity to return to her church and her people. Until now, she hadn't realized how deeply that desire was ingrained.

But she was only fooling herself. Being a

veterinarian was not what Amish women did. It was as simple as that.

Her anguish broke through with a sob.

Benjamin's heart leaped into his throat when he saw Abigail's tearstained face as she came staggering out of the bishop's house. He feared the worst—that she had been asked to leave—and in that moment he realized how much he had foolishly wanted this small, spunky woman to stay.

He wanted to kick himself for his interest in yet another ineligible woman. Would he never learn? What was behind his penchant for women straddling two worlds?

But self-recrimination would come later. Right now Abigail needed him, starting with the clean handkerchief he always kept in his pocket.

After a few minutes of walking silently by her side, she took a deep shuddering breath and mopped her face. "I'm sure you're burning up with curiosity about what happened," she observed with a bitter tinge to her voice. She twisted the scrap of cloth in her hands.

"*Ja*, sure," he acknowledged. "But not until you're ready to tell me."

She hiccuped, a childish sound, then related what the bishop said during the meeting. "In some ways, the meeting went worse than I thought it would," she concluded. "I know it was wrong of me, but I lost my temper."

"I'm sure that helped your case," he observed with some sarcasm.

"*Ja*, no doubt." She sniffed and stared down the road. "So now I have to make a choice— stay or leave. That's what it comes down to."

"That's pretty much as you thought it might be," he pointed out.

"*Ja*. I have some time to make up my mind, but in the end, I have to choose between my profession and my church." Her voice rose in frustration. "Is it such a bad thing, to be a professional?"

"You knew there would be consequences..." he began.

"*Ja, ja*, I know." She swiped at her eyes with an angry gesture. "But he makes it seem like it's something shameful or dishonorable. All I want to do is help animals."

"It's a cultural conflict," he admitted. "Of course, there's nothing shameful or dishonorable in being a vet. But you must admit, how many Amish veterinarians are there?"

"Okay, not many. But here's the thing—until I came back to take care of *Mamm*, I had forgotten a lot of what I cherished while growing up Amish. I realize now how much I want to stay, how much I want to be baptized. But I didn't tell that to the bishop. That's when I lost my temper. I told him I'd leave as soon as *Mamm* could spare me. I would turn my back on the community, and he wouldn't have to see me anymore. Then I stormed out."

"Real mature," he observed dryly.

He half expected her to explode with anger at his ill-timed quip, but instead she gave a bark of laughter. "*Ja*, I guess." She stooped down, picked up a stone from the gravel road and chucked it into the ditch, her movements clipped and angry.

"I wonder if the bishop is right," he mused. "It literally never occurred to me that your being back and fitting in so well might be a problem for *youngies*. I mean, that's kind of how you ended up becoming a vet, isn't it? Didn't you say a veterinarian made a strong impression on you when you were a *kinder*, after he cured one of your favorite cows?"

"*Ja*. But it's not like I wasn't interested in animals already by that age. It's just the first time I saw what someone could do with them."

"Then you must admit the bishop's concerns are valid. Every time you fix up an animal, you might be making some *youngie* wish they could do the same thing when they're older.

And wham, they've left the church community."

"If that's the situation, they would have left the church community anyway. Like your sister. Her calling to be a nurse was a higher calling than staying with the church."

He winced and felt the familiar knife twist in his midsection at the reminder of his losses.

"Maybe it would help if we explored the bishop's concerns."

She glanced at him. "Why?"

"Because potentially he's the one that holds your future in his hands."

She blew out a breath. "*Ja*, I guess. Sure, let's do it."

"Okay then. Let's say you open your vet clinic and treat a thousand animals a week." He saw her smile at his exaggeration, and pressed forward. "Suddenly you find yourself surrounded by admiring *youngies* who think it's wonderful that you went out into the *Englisch* world and became a vet, then came back and were baptized. What would you do under those conditions?"

"Hmm." He was pleased to see she looked thoughtful. "You mean, what would it be like if it seemed my dancing off to get a veterinarian degree didn't impact my future as a member of the church community? Is that it?"

"*Ja.* In short, having your cake and eating it, too. What the bishop sees is someone who did just that—who went out and became a professional, then came back and expected to be accepted by the community as if nothing out of the ordinary had happened. He's afraid if that's what you do—stay here and expect you can be baptized—then it will have an impact on the future of other *youngies*, who expect they'll be able to do the same thing."

"But that's what a *rumspringa* is all about—a chance for *youngies* to decide if they want to stay or go. It separates the wheat from the chaff."

"But you might say you were chaff when you left—and now if you decided to stay, you would want to become wheat. See what I mean?"

"*Ja,* I see what you mean," she said crossly. "But it's not like I'm a rock star or a celebrity. I just don't think that many *youngies* have a burning desire to do what I did. It was hard work, and being so far from family and all the support I grew up with sent me into despair a few times when things seemed bleak and I wasn't sure I could hack it. In other words, I don't think I'll be an influence one way or the other—neither positive nor negative. But those who want to leave the Amish should leave. Those who want to stay should stay."

Benjamin looked at her. It pained him to ask, but he did anyway. "And which category will you choose, to leave or to stay?"

She looked away. "I still don't know."

"That's what I thought." He fell silent as they neared his house. Suddenly he was anxious to get away from her.

The silence between them continued. Abigail's strides, which had been aggressive and angry, slowed. She paused a moment, met his eyes and said, "*Danke* for coming with me to the bishop's, Benjamin. It was…comforting."

She spun on her heel and walked away. He stared after her, wondering if she was taking his heart along with her.

Chapter Eight

Two weeks after her ill-dated interview with the bishop, Abigail watched her mother hobble from the table to the sink, where evening sunlight streamed through the western window and bathed the kitchen in a golden glow.

"Soon you won't need me," she observed. "I don't know how long it normally takes someone to recover from hip-replacement surgery, but you're back on your feet far sooner than I thought you would be, *Mamm*."

"*Nee*, I'm still slow." Esther started washing dishes. She insisted on doing this chore over Abigail's objections. "But it's not in my nature to let someone else take care of me. I'm grateful you're here, *liebling*, but it irks me to have you do all the kitchen work, especially since more and more people are asking you to look after their animals."

Abigail stretched her arms over her head. "*Ja*, it was busy today. My little clinic is hardly even furnished, but word is getting around. I'm glad I thought to bring a pet scale. Half the stuff I do involves knowing how much an animal weighs. I still have to refer about half of them to the clinic in town, though. I can't really do small-animal work without an X-ray machine."

"People seem to trust you—" Esther began, then broke off as she heard a pounding on the front door.

"Abigail?" called a voice she recognized as Benjamin's.

She strode over and yanked open the door. Benjamin stood panting on the porch.

"Lydia is in labor," he said without preamble. "Can you come?"

"*Ja*. Give me a moment to gather some supplies." Calmly, she selected a basket and began filling it with what she knew she would need to assist with a complicated whelping.

Benjamin fidgeted, and she noticed his agitation with some amusement. He was as twitchy as an impending father. "How long has she been in labor?" she asked.

"I noticed it a few minutes ago."

"Well, I know from experience it will take

some time before the first puppy shows up. Calm down, Benjamin."

He blew out a breath. "I know you're right. And this is her second litter. But the fact that she's going into this with both a cast on her leg and a cone around her neck makes me nervous."

"I'll get rid of that cone first thing." She picked up her basket and kissed her mother's cheek. "I don't know how late I'll be."

The evening shadows shaded most of the path between Esther's place and Benjamin's. He took the path at a fast walk, almost a jog, and she hurried to keep up with him.

"You said you noticed her a few minutes ago, but do you know how long she has been in labor?" she asked to his back.

He slowed fractionally and allowed her to catch up. "Probably a couple of hours. I'm kicking myself because I was working in the shop and left her in the house, and it wasn't until I went in that I noticed she was pacing up and down, limping on her healing leg. I have a whelping box I made for her, so as soon as I saw her behaving that way, I put her in the whelping box."

"*Gut.* That's a start. Classic nesting behavior. Have you taken her temperature?"

"*Nein.* I don't have a thermometer."

"I have one, so it will tell me something about how far along she's progressed."

Benjamin dashed up the porch steps and into the one-story log cabin. Abigail followed, clutching her basket of supplies.

The space Benjamin had arranged for his dog to birth her puppies met with Abigail's full approval—it was a large closet that had been emptied and lined with a secondhand baby-crib bumper, with a thick padding of thrift-store towels on the floor. The only disadvantage was the darkness—beneficial to the dog, no doubt, but inconvenient to a veterinarian.

Lydia was lying awkwardly amid these comforts, her battered plastic cone preventing her from behaving as a mother dog should. Abigail kneeled down next to the panting canine. "Let's get you out of this thing," she murmured, and untied the awkward barrier.

The moment the cone was off her neck, Lydia relaxed. She even licked Abigail's hand in apparent gratitude, then leaned down to sniff at the cast she had been unable to fully explore for the past few weeks.

While she was occupied, Abigail slipped in a thermometer. The dog hardly noticed.

"You'll have to light a lamp," she told Benjamin, who was hovering just outside the closet door. "I'll need to be able to see as things progress."

"*Ja*, wait a moment, I'll get one."

He returned with a lit kerosene lamp and inserted it into a shallow box mounted on the closet wall.

"Did you put that box there just for a lamp?" she asked in amazement, looking at the convenient bracket.

"*Ja*. This is the second time Lydia has used this closet as a whelping box. I needed light, too, but it was too dangerous to have an unsecured lamp in here, so I built the box to hold it."

"Clever." Abigail withdrew the thermometer and peered at the markings. "Ninety-eight-point-five," she noted. "Just right for a dog in labor."

She patted Lydia's head and stood up. "Let me unpack my supplies, and I'll need to see what you have for newborn puppies. But first, some calcium."

She spread out her supplies on the kitchen table and immediately loaded a plunger with a calcium gel, which she inserted into the dog's mouth before the animal could object.

"Calcium?" Benjamin asked. "What's that for?"

"Oral calcium," she clarified. "It helps guard against eclampsia, or milk fever, after whelping. Eclampsia is less common in large breeds, but it's nothing to mess around with. It also helps the whelping progress quickly and smoothly. Long, drawn-out birthings can stress the last puppies."

"She doesn't seem to mind the taste." He watched as Lydia literally smacked her jowls.

"It's supposed to give a nice aftertaste. Not that I've ever tried it myself," she added.

"How long before the puppies start coming?"

"Not for a couple hours at the least." She watched as he nervously fingered some colorful ribbons meant to identify each puppy at birth. "Do you want me to stay, or come back later?"

"I—I guess you can go," he said, pleating a ribbon.

Abigail knew he wanted her to stay but was reluctant to say so. She shrugged. "I don't have anything else going on, and I want to keep giving Lydia calcium as her labor progresses, anyway. You can keep me supplied with hot tea in exchange for my veterinary expertise."

He whooshed out a breath, and grinned. "*Danke!* And you can have all the tea you want!"

The moment lingered, until she grew nervous. She turned away from his compelling blue eyes. "Well, let's get things set up for when her labor becomes more active."

Besides the collection of ribbons, Benjamin had a scale, some iodine, sterilized scissors, stacks of old clean towels, hot water bottles and a notebook and pen. He also had a separate large basket lined with soft towels. Abigail knew he had prepared it to put the newborn puppies in until the whelping was finished, since mother dogs get restless between puppies. Having a separate basket for vulnerable newborns prevented accidental injury.

From far away, she heard Elijah bark, and the moo of a cow. "Do you need to do barn chores?" she inquired. "Milking cows or feeding chickens?"

He slapped his forehead. "*Ja*, I completely forgot. It won't take me long. I'll be back shortly." He scrambled out of the cabin.

Abigail watched him go, then bit her lip and decided to indulge in something she'd wanted to do for some time—explore his cabin. It was a charming, old-fashioned place, and she'd never seen it fully.

The kitchen was Spartan, with a wood cookstove and shelves instead of cabinets. The small living room was outfitted with comfortable furniture he no doubt had made himself. A large braided oval rag rug dominated the room, and she wondered who had made it. His mother, perhaps?

Off the kitchen was a large but mostly empty pantry. She peeked into his bedroom but did not enter. That was the whole of the cabin—kitchen, living room, pantry, bedroom. Eminently suitable for a bachelor, but she understood why other church members didn't want to live here. It would require a lot of work to expand for a growing family.

Within half an hour, Benjamin came in with two buckets of milk. "Any progress?"

"None." She watched him hoist the buckets onto the kitchen table. "Do you need help straining the milk?"

"*Nein*, I'm used to it."

He was right. Within minutes the fresh milk was poured into jars and placed in the icebox.

Outside, darkness fully descended. Crickets chirped. She heard the call of great horned owls—the deeper voice of the male at a distance, the higher-pitched call of his mate close by.

Benjamin lit another lamp, then a third, and the lighting gave the kitchen a cozy feel. Abigail felt like she was in an intimate bubble with Benjamin and the dog, separated from the outside world.

An hour went by, then two. Benjamin did indeed keep the kettle hot, and poured her a fresh mug of tea several times. He also kept a pot on the stove with hot, but not boiling, water for filling the hot-water bottles after the puppies were born. Lydia got out of the closet once or twice and took a restless turn about the room, then settled back into her nook. She shivered and panted, typical signs of a progressing labor. Abigail kept the animal well primed with calcium.

She felt the change in mood as the night progressed. Benjamin seemed very approachable, and she found herself talking with him as she'd rarely done with anyone else.

She told him about the time she'd gotten kicked by a horse, which had left a huge bruise on her leg.

In turn, Benjamin described his journey west to Montana. "I wasn't sure what to expect, but once I got here, I loved it."

Then Benjamin changed the subject to Mountain Days. "The festival liaison in town, a guy named Jonathan Turnkey, is optimistic that my demonstration will give a boost to my furniture-making business." Benjamin rubbed his chin. "I hope so. It's been something of an uphill battle for me."

Watching Benjamin's face in the lamplight, his eyes were shadowed and dark, but crinkled easily with humor. Up to this point, she'd regarded Benjamin with a reasonable amount of disinterest—as a kind and helpful neighbor, a solid member of the church—but that was it.

Now, for the first time, she reconsidered that. In the time since she'd been back with her mother, she learned everyone thought highly of him. He was a respected, trustworthy member of the community. In short, an eligible bachelor.

Yes, *he* might be eligible. The question was, was she?

Lydia's panting took on a more urgent tone. Peering close, she saw the dog was close to birthing her first pup.

"Go ahead and fill the hot-water bottles," she instructed Benjamin.

He hurriedly funneled hot water into the rubber containers, screwed the lids on tight and slipped them under the towels in the basket.

With soft groans, Lydia had the first puppy. Immediately Lydia turned and began vigorously licking the newborn, familiarizing herself with the puppy's scent. Abigail stayed vigilant so the new mother wouldn't accidentally hurt the baby with the clunky cast on her leg. The puppy made little mewing sounds. It was mostly white, with some large brown spots down its back and some pale brown markings around the eyes and ears.

It wasn't until Lydia began to birth the next puppy that Abigail carefully lifted the first baby out of the whelping box. She wiped its tiny nose and the inside of its mouth before placing it in the scale. "Fifteen-point-two ounces," she said. She peered at the baby's underside. "And a male. What ribbon color do you want for him?"

Benjamin selected a blue ribbon, which he tied around the baby's neck. Then he took the tiny animal, cuddled him for a few moments and placed him in the warmed basket. He noted the puppy's birth order, weight and ribbon color in the notebook.

Abigail turned her attention to Lydia, who had just had another puppy, which was a female.

The night wore on. Puppy after puppy arrived—eight, nine, ten, eleven...

"What an enormous litter!" she exclaimed. "I think Lydia is getting tired, poor thing." Holding a lamp close, concern gripped Abigail. "The next puppy is breech, with the tail coming first instead of the front paws," she told Benjamin. "I'm going to see if I can turn it. If I can't, we'll have to take Lydia into the vet clinic in town for an emergency C-section. I don't have the right equipment for that."

She saw his face turn pale. "Do what you can."

She had turned breech puppies before, and at least Lydia was a large breed with more room to work. Using the greatest care, she manipulated the puppy's position inside the mother, gently pushing and turning. She knew the signs of when a puppy would turn.

After a tense fifteen minutes, when she was getting cramped from bending over in such an awkward position, at last she felt the blessed movement she was hoping for—the puppy slid around nose-first. "Got it!" she breathed.

Lydia seemed to realize things were right. In a few minutes, the puppy was born.

"Boy," murmured Abigail. "And no wonder it was breech. Look how big he is."

But unlike the other puppies, who mewed and wiggled immediately after birth, this one was lying still and silent.

Abigail did what she could to help clear the puppy's nose and mouth, but the tiny body was unresponsive. "Not giving up," she muttered, and started massaging the newborn's underside. She covered the puppy's face with her mouth and blew into the lungs, and continued palpating the heart and lungs.

Lydia seemed concerned about the fate of the tiny animal in Abigail's hands. She whined and licked her hand. One minute passed, then two. Suddenly Abigail felt a twitch under her fingers. "C'mon, honey, come on…" she urged.

With a quick motion, the newborn puppy took its first breath. Abigail released her own breath, which she didn't realize she was holding. "He's all right." She grinned at Benjamin.

He grinned back, the tension whooshing out of the small whelping closet. For a moment Abigail was caught up in his eyes, made dark by the lamplight, but sparkling with gratitude… and something more.

Confused by her emotions, Abigail placed the puppy next to the mother dog's nose, and in seconds Lydia was greeting her latest newborn, licking him vigorously.

"I'm out of ribbons," commented Benjamin. "I didn't expect this many puppies."

Abigail palpated the mother's belly. "I think that's the last one, so he can be the only one without a ribbon. A dozen puppies! That's a lot for a dog this size." She gently poked the newest baby. "He's going to be a big boy, probably larger than his father. Look at his markings—three brown spots down his back and some markings on his face, like a mask."

"Badger marks, that's what they're called." Benjamin stood up and stretched after the cramped position on the floor. "Here, you must be tired." He reached down to help her up. "I can make more tea."

She put her hand in his as he assisted her to her feet. The moment lengthened as they stood together in the dark closet lit only by kerosene lamps.

He leaned in. "Abigail," he breathed, and lightly touched her lips with his.

Abigail's heart gave a lurch in her chest as she returned the kiss. For just a moment, she gave in to temptation. She felt a completion, a rightness...and then fear. Fear of her own weakness, her own longing. She pulled back. "B-Benjamin," she stuttered. "We can't."

He locked his hands behind the small of her back. "Maybe not, but it answers a question."

"Wh-what question?"

"Whether you felt the same as I did." He grinned.

She caught the impish light in his eyes and smiled back, but felt compelled to add a warning. "It'll never work out, Benjamin. I have too much uncertainty in my future."

"I know. I'm sorry. But you can't blame me for trying." He released her.

To cover her confusion, she turned to the basket containing the mewling newborn puppies. Her hands shook. "It's time to get them with their mother. They'll need to feed."

"Let me change the bedding first." Benjamin picked up the last-born puppy and handed it to Abigail, while he encouraged Lydia out of the closet.

Abigail held the tiny scrap of puppy, newborn-blind but now gloriously alive, and felt her heart melt. She'd never had a dog of her own and wondered if she would ever be settled long enough to have that luxury. She was aware Benjamin was working, but was lost in her own little bubble with the puppy.

"Guder daag?" Benjamin waved a hand in front of her face.

"I'm sorry." Abigail snapped out of her reverie. "I'm quite taken with this little guy. What a sweetheart."

"Let's start getting the other babies with their mama. I imagine they're hungry."

One by one, they transported the puppies with the rainbow of ribbons around their necks to the now-clean bedding underneath Lydia.

A yawn split her face. "What time is it?"

Benjamin held a lamp up to the clock on the kitchen wall. "Three in the morning."

"No wonder I'm tired. Still, the whelping went better than I anticipated. I'll keep the cone off Lydia's neck, but let me know if you see her chewing at her cast."

"I'll do that. And, Abigail… *Vielen Dank* from the bottom of my heart. I was so worried about her." He gestured toward Lydia, who was lying with a canine smile on her face and a pen full of puppies getting their first meal.

She smiled. "I'll check in with them tomorrow. Or rather, later today. Meanwhile, I'm off to get some sleep. I won't need a lamp, there's plenty of moonlight to see me home. *Gude nacht*, Benjamin."

She stepped out into the cool, moonlit night and started walking home. The pair of great horned owls that lived in the area boomed back and forth to each other. Abigail took deep, cleansing breaths and tried to calm herself.

Was she falling for Benjamin? She didn't want to. She'd fallen for someone before—hard—and it had turned out disastrously. Why, oh, why had her heart leaped when Benjamin kissed her? And why had she let her guard slip to reveal her emotions?

She rubbed her eyes, which were scratchy and tired from her all-night vigil with the dog.

Undoubtedly, the intimate setting had something to do with it.

Sparks had flown in that little closet setting. But she was as wrong for him as Barbara had been in his past. She was likely to return to the *Englisch* world soon enough. She didn't need to leave a trail of broken hearts behind as well—hers or Benjamin's.

She would aim to keep her interactions with him strictly professional from now on.

Benjamin watched Abigail's dim figure disappear into the moonlight. Then he wandered back in and looked at the young family in the whelping closet. The last pup born was the only one without a ribbon. He'd seen the love in Abigail's eyes as she held the tiny dog she had saved. Without Abigail's quick intervention, there would have been eleven puppies, not twelve.

He reached down and gently picked up the last pup born. It mewled and feebly pawed at being removed from the comfort of his mother and siblings. Benjamin cuddled the tiny animal, noting the faint markings around his eyes that would darken with age into a badger mask, which often characterized Great Pyrenees.

He was shaken by that moment he'd impulsively kissed her. So he wasn't the only one who had felt something between them.

He wondered if he should set himself *two* goals for the summer. The first was to organize the Mountain Days demonstration as the bishop had asked him. But he wondered if he could establish a second goal—to convince Abigail she should give up her aspirations to return to the *Englisch* world and instead stay here in Montana.

He looked down at the newborn litter. Every one of these puppies, in theory, already had a home. His waiting list for livestock guard dogs was long. But this little puppy...well, Benjamin was going to keep him.

Perhaps someday, the little puppy could be a wedding present for a bride. A bride who loved animals.

Chapter Nine

It was hard for Abigail to stay away from the litter of newborn puppies. She also knew she was using the puppies as an excuse to see Benjamin.

"I don't know what it is about this breed," she commented when the babies were three days old. She handed him his lunch hamper, then reached for the youngest puppy. "I've never spent much time around them, but they're beautiful. Aren't you?" She held aloft the still-blind animal. "I think this guy is my favorite."

"Well, you can legitimately say you saved his life. As for this lady…" He bent down and tousled Lydia's head. "She'll be mighty glad to have that cast off her leg."

"Three more weeks." Abigail cuddled the puppy to her chest. "I'm glad there were no post-whelping complications. What time are you leaving for the Herschberger farm tomorrow?"

It was the first barn-building Abigail had attended since she was a teenager, and she was looking forward to it...with the possible exception of seeing the bishop.

The church leader's ultimatum had disturbed her more than she thought. It's not as if he'd said anything she didn't anticipate. It's just that she still didn't know where her future lay. Her calling to practice animal medicine was still strong. But the longer she remained here, the stronger the pull she felt to return to her roots.

"Around seven in the morning," Benjamin replied. "Are you sure Esther is up for going? It's likely to be a long day."

"I doubt I could keep her away. This will be the first social function she's attended since her surgery, and I know every other woman there will keep her from lifting a finger. She's cooking up a storm right now. Speaking of which, I should get back and help. I don't want her overdoing it."

"I'll pick you up tomorrow at seven, then."

"Danke." Abigail took her leave and started walking back to her mother's cabin.

But something caught her eye. In the pasture

where Benjamin had his cows, several young calves gamboled about while their mothers rested in the shade, chewing their cud. But it wasn't the calves she noticed—it was a pair of coyotes at the far end, eyeing the babies with hunger in their eyes.

Those cows were part of Benjamin's livelihood. She had to warn him. Silently she retreated to the cabin and, without knocking, yanked open the door. "There are two coyotes in the field with your cows," she hissed.

Benjamin wasted no time. He strode out the door, grabbing his straw hat and jamming it on his head as he went. She ran after him.

But rather than approach the pasture fence, he motioned for her to hide herself behind a large tree while he did the same. "Watch," he advised.

"Watch?" she squeaked. "Those coyotes could take a calf, couldn't they?"

"Of course they could. Just watch." He gestured.

It was then that Abigail saw Lydia's mate, the Great Pyrenees dog named Elijah, silently gliding behind some trees along the fence line, straight toward the coyotes. Every previous time she'd seen the massive dog, he'd worn a goofy, happy expression. That expression was gone, and he looked grim—and dangerous—as he focused with laser intensity on the predators.

Her breath caught. She glanced at Benjamin, but he didn't seem worried. The cows chewed their cud and the calves frolicked about, oblivious to the presence of the hunters.

With a speed faster than she thought possible for a dog that size, Elijah raced full throttle at the coyotes, barking and snarling. The predators fled instantly, slipping under the fence and fleeing into the forest. The calves dashed toward their mothers. The cows snapped to their feet in alarm.

Elijah stared after the departing hunters, then turned and stalked back among his herd animals. She could almost see a smug expression on the dog's face.

She released a breath. "Impressive," she murmured.

"That's a Pyrenees for you," Benjamin replied. He stepped out from behind the trees and walked toward the fence, calling the large dog toward him. "Their first line of defense is barking, but they wouldn't hesitate for a moment to defend their herd more seriously if necessary. Their long fur protects them from teeth and claws of any predators they're fighting. That's a good boy..." he crooned, and gave the dog the accolades it deserved.

"I'm going to have to find out more about this breed," she commented, reaching over the top of the fence to join Benjamin in fussing over the dog. "There's just something about them I find fascinating."

"I feel the same way." He buried his hands in Elijah's fur. "They're powerful animals, and although they're perfectly capable of killing a predator, they prefer to act as a deterrent. That's why they're so barky. They're roamers, so they have to be confined to the field where their flock is, or they'll go off and patrol a much bigger territory. First thing in the morning, Elijah beats the boundary of this pasture and makes sure nothing has changed overnight."

"That's due to their independent nature, *ja?*"

"*Ja.* Above all, they're stubborn. They like to think for themselves, not blindly obey commands."

"And they're loyal." She tickled Elijah under the chin.

"Very loyal," Benjamin agreed. "They also work best in pairs. I've seen them do actual teamwork—one dog drawing a predator's attention while the other dog sneaks up from behind. But Elijah will be fine on his own until Lydia is able to join him again. Nonetheless, that's why I'm thinking on getting a second female. That way I can breed each one once a year while the other one stays teamed up with this big boy." He gave the dog a final pat on the head.

"I can see why so many church members are interested in herd guardians," she said. "There are a lot more predators out here in Montana."

"*Ja*, and all of us have livestock that's vulnerable."

"I can't wait to tell *Mamm* about this little bit of drama. She'll be impressed."

She finished her walk back to her mother's cabin. Esther was sitting at the table stirring a batch of cake batter. "I've decided to make cupcakes instead of a layer cake," she told Abigail. "Easier to handle."

"*Ja, gut. Mamm*, you'll never guess what I just saw…" Abigail described the incident with the coyotes while she started on some casseroles. "Great Pyrenees are magnificent animals," she concluded.

Abigail enjoyed afternoons cooking with her mother. It was something she'd missed after she'd left for school—the pleasant domestic bustle she'd taken for granted while growing up. She knew her mother missed her father fiercely at such times, since he was always the biggest fan of her cooking. Abigail wondered if her mother would ever remarry. Most

Amish didn't remain single for long after losing a spouse.

"Benjamin said he would pick us up at seven o'clock tomorrow morning." Abigail pushed a glass-lidded casserole dish into the oven. "He asked if you were up for going, and I said I couldn't keep you away."

Esther chuckled. "I've missed seeing everyone at the Sabbath services, so this is the next best thing. Besides, I understand another couple of families have moved here from Pennsylvania. Lois said her brother-in-law will be visiting as well. I haven't met any of the new arrivals yet. Here, *liebling*, I think these are ready to bake."

It wasn't until late evening that everything was cooked and baked to Esther's satisfaction. Abigail was tired, but didn't want to admit it in the face of her mother's industry.

"That should do it," Esther concluded at last.

Abigail wiped the last dish and put it away. "I'll get up early and have everything heated."

"Then let's go to bed," her mother advised. "We'll have a long day ahead of us tomorrow."

The next morning dawned bright and sunny. Abigail rose early and had everything heated and tucked in insulated carriers by the time Benjamin rolled up in his wagon.

"Ready, Esther?" he called as the older woman came out on the porch with her walker.

"Ja!" she called back cheerfully. "Let's go!"

Abigail carried the food to the wagon and nestled it among Benjamin's tools in the wagon box. Then she and Benjamin assisted Esther up into the wagon seat. The woman grunted once or twice in pain but otherwise climbed in with a dexterity that surprised her.

"It will be *gut* to see everyone," chattered Esther with childlike glee.

Abigail exchanged a grin with Benjamin over Esther's head.

"I know everyone's anxious to see you," he told Esther.

Soon, other wagons joined them on the road toward the Herschberger farm. Esther waved as people called greetings. Within a few minutes, Benjamin guided the horse up the gravel driveway and found a place to park. He hopped out and lifted Esther down from the wagon seat, then started unhitching the horse. "Do you need help going in?" he asked Abigail.

She shook her head. "We'll be fine," she told him. "Go build a barn."

He grinned—which momentarily took her breath away—then shouldered his tool belt and picked up a large wooden box of additional tools from the back of the wagon. She watched as he headed toward a cluster of men, who were busy planning the barn-raising strategy under the supervision of a foreman.

The barn's skeletal walls were already framed and lying on the ground, ready to be lifted into place. Soon teams would lift the walls into a vertical position using ropes and poles, and the barn would begin to take shape under their skillful hands.

It was a process she'd watched dozens of times during her childhood. It wasn't until she'd left the community and entered the *Englisch* world that she realized how rare the skill of carpentry was, and how few people used it.

Everywhere she heard the babble of voices and the shriek of children as they ran around the farm.

"*Komm, Mamm,* I'll settle you on the porch and then come back for the food." She made sure her mother was steady on her walker, and hovered nearby as Esther started moving over rough ground.

"Esther!" A woman's voice rose about the chatter. "Look, Esther is here!"

The older woman smiled as half a dozen of her friends descended upon her, chattering and asking questions.

Eva Hostetler wandered over, a smile on her

face. "*Gut* to see you here, Abigail," she said. "Your mother looks so much better."

"*Ja*, she is. And she was so looking forward to today." She watched as her mother, helped by solicitous hands, made her way to the house. "I think she's in *gut* hands. I'm going to grab the rest of the food."

"I'll help." Eva fell in beside Abigail as they returned to the buggy.

"Where's your *hutband* and children?" Abigail lifted a covered basket out and handed it to Eva, then reached in for the other.

"Daniel is busy with the men, of course. And Jacob and Mildred are somewhere, playing." She paused and a smile hovered on her lips. "And it seems we'll have a new *boppli* joining us in December or so."

"Oh, Eva…" Abigail stopped and stared at her friend, then threw an arm around her neck and gave her a hug. "That's wonderful!"

"*Ja*. I just pray things go well. I—I lost the last one early."

The smile dropped from Abigail's face. "I didn't know that. I'm so sorry."

"It was *Gott*'s will." The young mother sighed. "But it was harder than I thought it would be. It made me realize how precious our other two are and how much I like being a mother."

"I'll pray for you." Abigail realized how serious she was about the trite-sounding phrase. "Pray for a safe pregnancy and delivery."

"Danke." Eva took a deep breath and the smile flickered back on her face as she started walking again toward the house. "Don't tell anyone yet that I'm expecting, okay? I want to get a bit further along, at least until I'm showing."

"Don't worry, I won't." Abigail reached for the basket Eva was carrying. "But meanwhile I'll carry both baskets. I don't want you stressing yourself."

Eva chuckled and held the basket out of reach. "I have two active children. I'm always running around and carrying things. I think I can carry some baked goods. Now, how is the clinic going?"

Abigail walked toward the house and told her friend about the clinic's development. Once indoors, she unpacked the hampers amid the chattering women and felt a flush of warmth to be back within the camaraderie of the community.

She and Eva worked side by side, setting up tables and chairs, and laying out food and beverages while the din of hammers and saws dominated the barn-building area. She paused to watch. Benjamin stood braced with a pole in his arms, joining the other men to keep the first wall in place while the second wall was lifted to join it. She took a moment to appreciate the muscles in his arms as he strained to hold up the pole.

Eva came to stand beside her, watching the activity. "It should be a nice large barn," she observed.

"I've missed barn raisings," Abigail replied. "It's like the Bible verse says—one body with many parts, and each part has a different function, but together it makes a unified whole. Building a barn is almost like a dance, watching it all come together." Her gaze lingered on Benjamin. His shirt was already damp with sweat, and he joked and chatted with the men nearby. "But sometimes I feel like an outsider."

"There's Daniel." Eva pointed. "He's helping lift the second wall into place. How can you feel like an outsider? That's what you're doing with your veterinarian skills, aren't you? Contributing to the unified whole. Same with Benjamin, ain't so? He's using his skills to organize the Mountain Days demonstration."

"Reluctantly, *ja*."

"Reluctant or not, he seems to be doing a *gut* job. I've heard a number of people talking about how they can make their particular demos more interesting and interactive. I think people are pretty excited about it, to be honest."

"That's *gut* to hear!"

With the second wall in place and secured, she saw Benjamin remove his pole and begin working on a cross girt. Abigail turned back to help the other woman with lunch preparations. Walking next to Eva, she noticed an *Englisch* man pull up in a car and exit the vehicle. He walked over toward where the men were working and stood, watching. He seemed very much out of place in his plaid shirt, blue jeans and cowboy hat.

"Look." She pointed. "Who's that?"

Released from bracing the pole, Benjamin fished a handkerchief out of his pocket and mopped his face. Then he slipped his favorite hammer out of the loop on his tool belt and prepared to work on the cross girts.

Then he noticed the *Englisch* visitor, looking as out of place as a petunia in an onion patch. Benjamin suppressed a sigh. The man was none other than Jonathan Turnkey, the liaison for the Mountain Days celebration in the town of Pierce. Benjamin liked the *Englisch* man well enough, but he had work to do.

Slipping his hammer back into the loop on his tool belt, Benjamin strode over and assumed a cheerful demeanor. "Good morning, Jonathan!"

"Good morning." Jonathan shook Benjamin's hand. "I heard a rumor a barn was going up and had to see if for myself."

"*Ja*, this one is for the Herschberger family. We're trying to get a barn built for everyone who needs one before winter."

"A good goal." Jonathan's eyes rested on the activity. "What a pity you couldn't demonstrate something like this for Mountain Days."

Benjamin chuckled. "It would be hard to organize. What would we do with the barn once it was built? It's not like we could leave it in the field at the fairgrounds."

"Well, actually, you probably could. But in that case it would become a public building, and if it's not built exactly to code, all the bureaucrats would have a fit."

"So bureaucrats plague you, too?"

"Oh, yeah. They plague everyone." Jonathan gestured toward the activity. "I know there's a lot to do before sunset, but can you show me around?"

For the briefest moment Benjamin thought about refusing. The man was right—they had a lot to do before sunset, and taking the time to show an *Englisch* visitor around would only slow things down. But Benjamin knew the goodwill of the church and the success of the demonstrations hinged to some degree upon Jonathan, and he changed his mind.

"*Ja*, sure," he said. "But you'll excuse me if I don't take long? Every pair of hands is needed."

Some of the men working on the structure gave Jonathan wary nods as Benjamin walked him around, but Benjamin was careful not to let him engage anyone in conversation and slow down the work. And he blessed the man for not pulling out a camera to document everything, which was increasingly common in encounters with the *Englisch* in town.

Instead he discussed the method of barn construction used by the church community. "This technique was used in pre-industrial America," he told Jonathan. "The skeletal sides you see are called 'bents.' We make them ahead of time, constructing them where they lay. We lift them into place using ropes and poles, then use cross girts as horizontal framing members connecting the end posts beneath the roof plate."

He walked slowly with Jonathan, pointing out how the horizontal tie beams would be connected between the feet of each pair of rafters in the roof structure, and then fastened to the end posts below the roof plate. "We build temporary scaffolding and lay it across the horizontal beams so we can work at higher elevations."

"No premade trusses," observed Jonathan.

Benjamin lifted his eyebrows. "You sound like you know construction."

"Of course. My dad worked in construction all his life."

Benjamin smiled. "Then we speak the same language. You're right, we don't use premade trusses, which are often required by code. But our barns are sturdy and well-made, and will last for generations." He noticed a flurry of activity at another of the bents lying on the ground. "I'm needed to help lift the next side into place. I'm sure the bishop won't mind if you stay and watch."

Jonathan nodded. "Thank you, I will. And I promise to keep out of the way."

With a smile, Benjamin rejoined the men and prepared to help lift the third wall of the barn into place.

But he was more self-conscious than before, aware of a strange pair of eyes upon the scene. From the more subdued chatter of the men, he knew they were also more self-conscious.

He knew many townspeople were interested in how the church community did things. But the church did things the way they did because it was traditional, not because it was quaint.

They didn't do it to show off. That would be *hochmut*.

Yet here, in what should have been an ordinary barn raising, he suddenly felt like they were showing off for the *Englisch* observer. It was an uncomfortable feeling, like being an exhibit in a zoo. Still, if the bishop didn't have an issue with it, neither could he.

By lunchtime, he was ready for food and a break. The women had set up tables under the shade of trees. Jonathan had fallen into conversation with some of the grandfathers whose bodies were too old to work construction, but who had come to the event for the social opportunities. The older men sat in chairs, canes clasped in front of them, and chatted amiably with the visitor. Benjamin felt grateful to the graybeards.

"Who is that?"

He glanced over and saw Abigail, a covered casserole dish in her hands. She had a sheen of sweat on her forehead from working in the hot kitchen. She jerked her head toward Jonathan.

"His name is Jonathan Turnkey," he told her. "He's my liaison with the town's Mountain Days event. He'd heard we were having a barn raising and came to see what it was all about."

"You don't like him?" Her voice held a note of surprise.

"*Nein*, I like him just fine. But it kind of changed the atmosphere among the men when he showed up. Everyone became a bit more self-conscious, I noticed."

"*Ja*, I understand that." She pushed a wisp of hair away from her eyes. "I was always being watched, especially when doing farm calls. A lot of people don't think women can make *gut* livestock vets, especially a small woman like me. I was always being judged while on the job." She placed the casserole dish on a table and wiped her hands and then her forehead with her apron. "How long is he staying? Will he be joining us for lunch?"

"I don't know…"

"Well, he's welcome if he wants to stay."

He looked at her in some amazement. "You really don't mind, do you?"

"Mind what?"

"Having an *Englischer* join us for lunch at a barn raising."

"*Nein*. Why should I?" Her expression altered a bit as she looked at him. "Benjamin, don't forget—I spent ten years living and working as an *Englisch* woman. I like them. And you said you liked this Jonathan Turnkey, *ja*? So go ask if he's staying for lunch."

"I wonder if I'll ever develop your easiness," he mused. "You're like a chameleon. Very adaptable."

She chuckled. "You might say I went through two schools when I left the community—veterinarian school, and the school of hard knocks. I had to learn to be *Englisch* in a hurry, and I found it wasn't so bad."

"And now that you're back, have you decided which world you want to live in?"

Her serene expression disappeared and a scowl took its place. "*Nein.* And don't push me, Benjamin. I'm not ready to make up my mind yet."

"As you say." He turned to look over at Jonathan, who seemed perfectly at ease among the graybeards. "Well, I suppose I'll go ask if he wants to stay for lunch."

He watched as Abigail walked back toward the chattering women, admiring her figure, then grinned to himself. He liked her spunk.

Feeling better about Jonathan's presence, he went to talk to the *Englisch* man.

Chapter Ten

When Abigail went to remove Lydia's cast three weeks later, she found Benjamin in an unusually jubilant mood.

"Guess what!" he sang as she approached his front porch, with her vet tools in hand. "I was able to convince Luke Fisher to demonstrate grain grinding at the Mountain Days demo next week!"

Abigail smiled. "You've been wanting that for a long time. What convinced him?"

"I suspect his wife, but I was too smart to ask." He gave her a triumphant grin that nearly buckled her knees. "That's the last member of the church community I'm going to ask. We have so many demos, we could practically have our own stand-alone fair."

"I like how the bishop took your idea and turned the last 'barn raising' into a 'booth raising,'" she observed. "Now it seems everyone will have a handsome place to demonstrate their skills and sell their wares. You said you're going to have a whole booth for your furniture?"

"*Ja*, and I've half built some chairs and a table so I can show people how it's done. I'm also having order forms printed up in case someone wants to place an order."

"*Mamm* has been joining the other women for the last week sewing up bunting and banners to make everything look colorful and welcoming. She mentioned she was making bunting for your booth."

"That's *gut* of her. It's like the whole church is throwing itself into this with a lot more enthusiasm now."

Abigail noticed how his dark blue eyes twinkled, and the dimples that bracketed his mouth were showing more often. She had been thinking about those dimples a great deal lately, especially after that night when the puppies were born. Their kiss still lingered in her mind.

She pulled her thoughts together. "You, too," she told him. "You seem to be enjoying yourself?"

"*Ja*." His grin faded into a thoughtful expression. "I guess I am. It's nice to see it all coming together. Are you still interested in helping set things up next week?"

"*Ja*, of course. I wouldn't miss it for anything."

"Then I may ask if you could work in my booth. I'll be doing a chair-making demo and have some pieces for sale, as well as forms for orders. But I'll also be acting as the information booth, so having an extra person to answer visitors' questions would be helpful."

Abigail's heart leaped at the thought of spending the whole day in Benjamin's company. "Of course. In fact, I'm probably your best bet for answering questions since I have both the *Englisch* and the Amish perspective. How's business?" she added, knowing he had been concerned about his finances.

Benjamin grimaced. "Slow. That's why I'm hoping the fair will give me more exposure and bring in orders. If it doesn't, I'll have to go to work for someone this fall. I prefer to work for myself, but..." His voice trailed off.

Abigail knew by now how much he valued his independence. "You're so skilled," she assured him. "I can't imagine you'd have a problem finding a job."

"I know you're right. I just like working at my own pace, in my own shop. Sometimes I wonder..."

"Wonder what?" she prompted as he gazed into the middle distance.

He snapped back to the present. "Sometimes I wonder if I shouldn't have migrated out here. My business was thriving in Indiana. Here, it takes time to build up customers. I'm bringing in some income by providing dairy products to the Yoders' store, but since dairy farming isn't my full-time job, the income isn't enough to keep me going. I may be pinning too much hope on how much of a jump start this demonstration may give me." He sighed. "Sometimes I think I should give up woodworking altogether and stick to cows."

"I'm not a financial expert," warned Abigail. "But diversifying your income seems smart to me. You have both the cows and the furniture business. When one is slow, you can ramp the other up, and vice versa."

"You're right." Benjamin scrubbed a hand over his face, then quirked a lopsided smile at her. "I'm sorry, I didn't mean to dump my worries on you."

"That's what friends are for, ain't so?" Abigail smiled back. "Meanwhile, let's see how Lydia's getting along."

The magnificent white dog thumped her tail when Abigail approached, and seemed only too happy to escape the closet with her litter of puppies, still all adorned with a rainbow of ribbons around their necks. The babies' eyes were open and they were moving around on their feet, comically unsteady. Abigail grinned at her favorite little animal, the youngest puppy whose life she had saved.

"Time enough to cuddle him later," she murmured, before turning her attention to the mother.

It took some time to remove the cast using the battery-powered cast saw and cast-spreader tool, and Lydia remained placid throughout. "I've never seen such a calm dog," she remarked to Benjamin, who sat on the floor with his pet's head on his lap. "It's like she knows her ordeal is over."

"They're smart, these Pyrenees," he remarked. He stroked Lydia's thick ruff. "She's never fought you during everything you've done for her."

"How easy are these dogs to train?" She worked her way through the cast.

"It depends on what you mean by 'train,'" he replied. "If you mean the usual 'sit, stay, come, roll over' that people teach their dogs, they're terrible. Pyrenees are bred for independent thinking, not mindless obedience. But they can work cooperatively and protect entire flocks of any livestock you put in their care."

"Impressive." She noticed how Lydia watched the process taking place with her leg with stoic interest but no panic. "Then maybe she *does* know her ordeal is over."

Abigail finally was able to peel back the halves of the hard casing around Lydia's leg, and she began removing the padding. "This is going to feel *so* much better," she crooned to the dog. "You've been such a *gut* girl, not chewing on your cast even without a cone on."

At last the animal's leg was free of the obstruction. Lydia leaned down and sniffed at the shaved skin that had been covered up for so many weeks. Then she rolled to her feet and took a tentative step. Then another. Then another. Then she turned, walked up to Abigail and gave her a kiss.

Abigail's heart melted at the dog's gesture. She pulled the animal toward her by her ruff and pressed her forehead to the dog's forehead. For a moment she felt a communion with the animal before the canine pulled away and returned to the closet to attend to her puppies.

"That was amazing," breathed Benjamin.

"What?" She looked over to see him staring at her.

"I've never seen her behave that way toward anyone. It's like she was thanking you."

"Well, you're the one who said they're smart dogs."

"*Ja.* Maybe I didn't realize just *how* smart."

"Time for me to see my favorite puppy." Abigail reached into the closet and fished out the ribbonless male. "Goodness, he gets cuter every time I see him."

"You should give him a name."

"Why?" With sudden dismay, Abigail put the puppy down, and he wobbled back toward his mother. "A name implies permanence, and I'm not here permanently."

Why did she see a small tug of amusement at the corners of Benjamin's mouth? "Well, regardless, I can't thank you enough for your care of Lydia. Look at her! Except for the shaved fur on her leg, you'd never know it was broken."

"*Gut.*" Abigail repacked her veterinary supplies. "Well, I'm off. *Mamm* is hosting a sewing circle again this afternoon to work on bunting, though I think that's just an excuse to have some women over to visit."

Abigail walked back to her mother's cabin, thinking about Lydia and the puppies…and their owner. Lately Benjamin was becoming far too easy to talk to and work with. He was a comfortable man. A handsome man. Despite his financial concerns, he seemed to be more at peace lately. Maybe the bishop was right to give Benjamin this task, perhaps knowing it might help him expand his business. The bishop was a wise man.

She scowled at the ground. Wise, yes. But the church leader was still implacable when it came to her own future. She knew she had to choose: whether to remain a vet and leave her church, or abandon her career and stay.

Her mother was approaching the point where she could live independently again. Soon Abigail would have to make up her mind about whether to stay or leave.

"*Gott*, show me Your will," she prayed in what was becoming an alarmingly frequent petition. So far her prayers had not been answered.

Back in the cabin, Abigail packed away her vet supplies, gave the house a quick dusting and set out a series of folding chairs. Her *mamm* had made some blueberry cheesecake tarts, which were now chilling in the icebox.

Abigail snitched one of the treats. "Do you sell these at the Yoders' store?" she asked, her mouth filled with the sweet creamy taste.

"*Ja.* They're quite popular."

Abigail swallowed. "I can see why. You always were the best pastry chef, *Mamm*."

Esther's face creased into a grin. "You always did have a sweet tooth, *liebling*."

Impulsively Abigail leaned down and kissed her mother on the cheek. "For sure and certain, it's been nice spending time with you."

A knock at the door interrupted the sentimental moment. Abigail answered, and within a few minutes the house was swarming with smiling, chattering women, their arms full of colorful fabrics.

Esther held court from her favorite chair, and Abigail served iced tea and the tarts. But the women had come to sew, and after the treats were finished, they settled in with needles and thread.

"I'm going to wrap these around the booth poles," said one woman, holding up her solid green fabric. "I have yellow and blue swags as well, so that will catch the eye."

"Do you think I should wrap my poles, too?" asked another woman. "I was going to have skirting on the tables, and wrapping poles in fabric might be too much."

Listening to the discussions, Abigail smiled. Most of the women had never displayed anything. The Amish stricture against pride— *hochmut*—was so ingrained, it was challenging to step outside their comfort zone and think in terms of what would attract the eyes of visitors…especially *Englisch* visitors.

While many of the church women had their own smaller booths for demonstration and sales, a large number were participating in a demo of one of their best-known skills, quilt-making. Benjamin had recommended at least three large quilting frames, and Esther had volunteered to act as spokeswoman, explaining to visitors how hand-quilting was done as a team project and how the designs were created.

Abigail herself—having no particular skill worth demonstrating—kept her plan to work the information side of Benjamin's booth.

The Friday before the Mountain Days festival dawned warm and lovely. Benjamin rose early, full of nervous energy. Today, nearly the entire church community would join him in setting up the demonstration area. Tomorrow was the event itself. After so many months of planning, it was hard to believe the moment was finally here.

He made sure Lydia and her puppies had plenty of fresh food and water as well as outdoor access, since he would be gone most of the day. He smiled at the wobbly male puppy Abigail adored. He hoped that, someday, she would accept the gift of the puppy to have as her own.

After loading his wagon full of tools, he swung into the seat, clucked to the horse and drove toward Abigail's cabin to pick her up.

She was waiting for him, a hamper of lunch in hand. *"Guder mariye,"* she said as she climbed into the seat next to him. "Nervous?"

"How did you know?" He gave her a grin as he directed the horse toward town. "I hardly slept last night."

"It will be all over tomorrow afternoon. Meanwhile you've worked so hard, planning every last detail, I can't possibly see how it can fail."

"I hope you're right."

He was mostly silent as they clip-clopped toward the outskirts of Pierce, where the fairgrounds were located. He thought he would arrive before anyone else, but to his surprise the bishop and two other families were already there, measuring out their designated demonstration area. Additionally, a slew of *Englisch* townspeople were swarming over the fairgrounds setting up carnival rides and finalizing the display halls for photography, artwork and garden produce.

"Guder mariye!" he called to the bishop. He pulled the horse to a stop and jumped out.

"I've got stakes and ribbons for marking booth locations."

"Ja, gut," Bishop Beiler replied. *"Guder mariye,* Abigail. Are you helping set up?"

"Ja." She climbed down from the wagon and said no more.

The day passed quickly. Benjamin consulted with Jonathan Turnkey, the event coordinator, to make sure the demonstration area was being set up correctly, but after that the Amish were mostly left to themselves.

More and more families arrived, and the air soon rang with sounds of hammers and chatter. Benjamin noticed how the men concentrated on putting up the infrastructure, but it was the women who gave the spaces touches of home. Beyond bunting and banners and flagging, he saw tablecloths, baskets and other domestic props.

Small groups of townspeople setting up their own displays often wandered through to see what the Amish group was doing. Benjamin noticed a lot of intergroup chatting as both Amish and *Englisch* became acquainted with each other. He heard lots of laughter.

At noon, people broke for lunch, spreading quilts on the grass and opening hampers of cold chicken and macaroni salad. Abigail sat with Eva Hostetler and her family while he found himself seated with the bishop.

"Benjamin, this is turning out very well," the bishop said, biting into a chicken leg. "I must say, you've done an excellent job."

The rare praise made Benjamin pause. He hardly knew what to say, but finally settled on a simple response. *"Danke."* Then honesty prompted him to add, "I'll be glad when it's over."

"Ja, me, too. But this should establish us as strong partners with the *Englisch* in town. We took for granted the ties we had in Indiana, but here, we're starting out new. No longer will we be seen as standoffish or remote. We can be seen as neighborly and helpful. Cooperative."

"I suppose. The best part is, as always, the camaraderie of working with the whole church community on a common goal."

The bishop laid down his chicken leg. "And you, Benjamin. Has working on this project helped you overcome your aversion to the *Englisch*?"

"So that *is* the reason you gave me this assignment." He quirked a smile at his church leader.

"Ja, of course." The older man spoke as if the conclusion was obvious. "You were eaten up with bitterness inside over decisions made

by other people. You were blaming those who were blameless. I hoped this would help."

"I won't say I'm cured, but I suppose this project helped." Never would he admit the biggest reason behind the shift in his attitude was Abigail.

Petite little Abigail, now sitting and chatting so demurely with Eva, had changed his mind about many things. He knew he was pinning hopes on a future with her, but he also knew he didn't dare tell her until such time as she had made up her mind about what she wanted to do.

Benjamin was a patient man. He would wait.

Work resumed after lunch. By the time the evening shadows loomed over the fairgrounds, the demo area was finished—booths had been set up, display areas were cordoned off and temporary corrals were enclosed. Each stand had a sign politely asking visitors to refrain from photography, though he knew that request was likely to be ignored.

He called the group together before departing. "Those of you bringing animals will need to be here especially early," he said. "All buggies and wagons should be parked there—" He pointed toward a roped-off area. "All horses, except the draft horses, can be let loose in that field. It has plenty of shade and I'll make sure the water tubs stay full. Those bringing draft horses and milk cows already have your areas set up."

He continued giving instructions and receiving input, and within half an hour everyone seemed satisfied.

"Okay, let's go home," he concluded. "We have a long day ahead of us tomorrow."

As he hitched up his horse to the wagon, Abigail joined him. She was smiling, and it was hard to admit the leap within him at her dancing brown eyes.

"This is going to go very, very well," she said as she climbed onto the wagon seat.

"I hope so. I alternate between elation and despair. Elation, because everyone seems enthusiastic. Despair, because it's something I've never done before, and this is—to borrow a phrase from the *Englisch*—where the rubber meets the road." He climbed up beside her and clucked to the horse.

"You've been obsessing over every detail for so long that I can't imagine there's anything you've overlooked," she assured him. "Relax, Benjamin. You might be in charge, but it's very much a group project. Everyone can work at setting up his own booth space or demonstration area. And the people in town have been so kind and helpful."

"Yes they have," he admitted. "I'll admit, it was enjoyable watching the fair staff mingle with the church participants. Everyone seemed to get along."

"It will go well, Benjamin. Don't worry."

"I appreciate that you'll be helping answer questions in my booth tomorrow."

"It works out perfectly since I don't have any special skills I could demonstrate."

He laughed out loud at that. "No special skills? Except for setting broken bones on dogs or stitching up cow udders or helping a pig farrow."

She chuckled. "Maybe, but I can hardly demonstrate that to a crowd, can I? No, as far as everyone is concerned, tomorrow I'm not a vet. I'm just a church member, that's all."

Back home that evening, Abigail helped her mother wash dishes. "I think everything is packed for tomorrow," she told Esther. "You sure you don't mind if I'm in the information booth instead of with the quilters?"

"*Ja*, sure. I'll just send all the nosiest people toward you." Esther chuckled. "Unlike you, I'm not so easy with the *Englisch* that I could spend all day answering questions. But as the bishop said, I'm looking at tomorrow as an educational opportunity. Not many people in Montana know about our church."

"I think you'll be surprised how much interest there will be," Abigail replied. "Just get used to the fact that a lot of people will ignore the No Photography signs."

Esther pointed to a large duffel bag near the door. "Why are you bringing so many veterinarian supplies?"

"Just as a precaution." Abigail dried a dish. "With so many farm animals at the demo, it's wise to be ready. I'll keep the bag in the information booth. Benjamin's nervous," she added. "I think that's half the reason he wants me in the booth to answer questions. I told him I had more experience dealing with the *Englisch* and their questions, so it might calm him down if I was there."

Esther paused in her work and looked at Abigail. "You like him, don't you?"

"Ja." Abigail knew exactly what her mother was asking. She rinsed a dish. "I suppose I do. But it makes no difference. The bishop made it clear what my choices are. I'm not ready to give up the gift *Gott* gave me, *Mamm.* The gift of working with animals. Since that means I won't be allowed to be baptized into the church, it would be cruel to toy with Benjamin's affections. I won't do it."

Esther sighed. "I was hoping to see my youngest child settled someday…"

"Mamm." Abigail allowed a ghost of a smile to cross her face. "Your youngest child hasn't been settled since she was eight years old. It's a different lifestyle I've chosen, but it's not a bad one."

"Perhaps not. But I don't see you as happy, *liebling.* I think that's what worries me. When you came back from your work as a vet in Indiana, you looked shell-shocked somehow. Maybe the work was too hard, I don't know. All I know is you've blossomed since you came here."

Abigail knew she had been troubled because of her terminated romantic interest in Robert, her boss. But Esther didn't know about that… and hopefully never would.

She handed her mother the last dish for drying. "We'd best get an early night. Benjamin is picking us up at the crack of dawn. I hope I can sleep tonight. I think I've picked up on some of Benjamin's nervous energy."

"Everything will go well," Esther predicted. "What could possibly go wrong?"

Chapter Eleven

The day of the town celebration dawned bright and clear. The weather promised to be warm, but not hot.

"What a gift," Benjamin called out as he helped Esther onto the wagon seat. "I know everyone in town was hoping that the weather would hold."

"Did you get any sleep last night at all?" teased Abigail, swinging her bag of veterinarian supplies into the back of the wagon.

"Not a whole lot," he admitted. "I kept imagining a raft of things that could go wrong."

With Esther occupying the more comfortable wagon seat, Abigail climbed into the wagon box and seated herself on a pile of feed sacks. "Just remember, the bulk of your work is done. At this point, everyone participating is responsible for his own demonstration."

"I know. It's just that I feel…" He gestured. "Accountable."

"There's no Sabbath service tomorrow," she told him. "It's an off-Sunday, so you can sleep until noon if you like."

"And I might just do that. Look." He pointed. "We're not the only ones getting an early start."

In fact, as they made their way toward town, Abigail noted quite a number of wagons heading in the same direction. She saw three separate farmers walking, leading well-brushed Jersey milk cows for the milking demonstration. She saw another two sets of men with bridles of draft horses in hand, leading the massive equines for the plowing demonstration. The animals' coats gleamed.

"Is there anyone *not* participating?" she wondered out loud. "I mean, seriously, even if a church member doesn't have a specific skill to demonstrate, it looks like everyone's showing up simply for support." Her heart swelled at the thought.

"I honestly can't think of anyone who wanted to be left behind." Benjamin lifted an arm to wave at someone. "Like you, Esther—even the older crowd is coming to join with quilting or cooking or to keep an eye on the kids or something."

"I know it's *hochmut* to admit, but it makes

me proud to be part of this group." Abigail spoke quietly. "I grew up taking for granted the number of everyday skills and talents within the community. It wasn't until I left to go to school that I realized how fascinated the wider world is in those skills. I have a feeling today is going to be very popular."

By the time the fair had officially opened and the first wave of *Ensglisch* visitors strolled through, the Amish demonstration section was fully staffed and underway. Many people had wares for sale, and sales were brisk. But the skills on display—basket weaving, butter churning, quilting, leather working and endless other occupations—were popular beyond words.

As the day went on, the crowds grew thick. Very thick.

In one large field, two sets of draft horses were fully harnessed and resting in the shade of large pine trees. Once an hour, the farmers hitched them to a cultivator and showed viewers how they directed the massive teams of horses across the fields.

In another area, four placid dairy cows with doe eyes and fawn-colored fur were on display. People were invited to sit down on the stools and learn how to milk them.

Under the shade of three separate canopies, quilting frames had been set up, and a large number of women were grouped around, sewing busily, answering questions to curious onlookers. Quite a few *Englisch* women were allowed to join in, with neighboring Amish women showing them how to guide the needle through the top of the fabric with their dominant hand and redirect it from below with their nondominant hand. Meanwhile dozens of colorful quilts were displayed for sale.

Two women who were expert basket weavers showed interested visitors what kinds of materials they used and how they prepped them for working. Children and adults alike were invited to try their hand at manipulating the softened branches and other materials into the beginnings of baskets. Finished baskets sold briskly.

The leather workers had brought along hides in various stages of completion, and Eva's father, Eli, showed how he fashioned bridles and reins from the finished pieces, riveting the leather and making the ribbons supple.

In each demonstration area, a prominent sign discouraged photography, but a large number of people ignored the suggestion and recorded the church members at work. The bishop had already warned the church members of this likelihood, and advised them to gracefully ignore the actions.

Benjamin's booth featured two signs—one for his furniture, the other for visitor information. Abigail, stationed on the information side, answered questions almost nonstop. She was gratified to see a great deal of interest in Benjamin's construction techniques, and saw more than one person fill in a form for a future order.

But it wasn't until afternoon when things took a turn for Benjamin. Esther left her post with the quilters and hobbled over on the arm of an unknown Amish man of about her age, trailed by another *Englisch* man who had the look of a businessman about him.

"*Mamm*, are you okay?" asked Abigail in some alarm.

"*Ja*, I'm fine." The older woman had some high color in her cheeks. "This is Mark Beiler, the bishop's brother, who's visiting from Indiana. Mark, this is my youngest daughter, Abigail."

A bit confused, Abigail shook the older man's hand and greeted him politely.

Esther then turned to the *Englisch* man. "Mark wanted us to meet this gentleman, Greg—Greg… I'm sorry, what did you say your last name was?"

The *Englisch* man stepped forward. "Greg Anderson, ma'am." He shook Abigail's hand. "I own a large construction firm specializing in log homes. I have a branch office in Indiana, which is how I know Mark. Your mother suggested I might be interested in the furniture made by this young man." He tilted his head at Benjamin, who was involved with a customer and barely noticed the new arrivals.

"He's busy at the moment, as you can see," Abigail replied, "but if you'll have a seat, I'm sure he'd be very interested in talking with you. In fact, you'll be able to sample how comfortable his chairs are." She gestured toward one of Benjamin's specialty rocking chairs.

Esther turned. "I'll head back to the quilters now."

With Mark Beiler solicitously at her elbow, Abigail watched in some bemusement as her mother limped away.

Her attention was diverted by several *Englisch* women, who descended *en masse* on the booth with questions, but she was aware of Benjamin behind her, greeting the newcomer. He showed the visitor the variety of furniture he made, and the man flipped through a photo catalog of the various pieces that Benjamin specialized in. But she was so occupied that she couldn't catch much of what was being said until Mr. Anderson walked away, clutching a catalog and a business card.

For a few more busy minutes, the booth was swamped with visitors. Benjamin joined her in answering questions. People were genuinely eager to know more about the Amish lifestyle, how they'd ended up in Montana and the specific skills being demonstrated.

And then, as if from some hidden signal, the crowds around the booth dissipated as people wandered in different directions, and she and Benjamin had a rare moment of peace.

"Whew." She slumped against the booth's side and gulped some water. "I never expected it to be this busy."

"Did you hear what happened with Greg Anderson?" Benjamin's smile was broad, and he nearly quivered with happiness.

"No, what happened?"

"He wants a standing order of furniture!" he burst out. "He owns a huge log-home business with branch offices in many states, and he likes my furniture so much he wants to showcase it in many of his display homes. He said that could amount to hundreds of pieces of furniture!" Abigail gasped when he suddenly swept her up in a hug and spun her around.

She laughed from the pure joy of being in his arms before remembering they were in public. She stepped back and returned his grin. "I'm so glad for you! *Gott ist gut!*"

"*Ja*, and when…"

He broke off as screams could be heard from one of the nearby fields. He jerked around and stared. Abigail heard dog growls mingled with cries of horror.

Instinctively she reached for her duffel bag of veterinarian supplies when a teenage Amish boy ran up to the booth. "Abigail!" he gasped. "A dog—it's attacked one of the dairy cows. There's blood. Can you come?"

"*Ja.*" She jerked the duffel strap over her shoulder and raced after the teen. She feared the worst. She'd seen cows savaged by dogs before, and it would haunt her if she had to put a beautiful milk animal down, and in front of a crowd, too.

A circle of people, both *Englisch* and Amish, pressed around the milking demonstration area. One of the beautiful Jerseys stood trembling and injured. The owner, a man named Ephraim King, stood at the cow's head, holding her halter and trying to soothe the injured animal. An *Englisch* woman crouched at the edge of the demo area, weeping in remorse, her arms around the large dog that had savaged the cow.

"I'm so sorry," she gabbled. "He's never seen

a cow before. He just broke away from me. I'm so sorry, I'm so sorry…"

Abigail pushed her way to the front of the crowd and kneeled before the cow. "Hold her halter tight," she told Ephraim. He nodded and regripped the lead rope.

She dropped her duffel and unzipped it until she found some antibacterial wipes, which she used to wipe the wound clean. The first thing she had to do was see how injured the animal was. The onlookers fell into a respectful silence as she worked.

She could feel the cow tremble beneath her hands. She saw teeth marks, and a rip in the cow's tough skin about four inches long.

"Quite a dog," she muttered. While she sympathized with the visitor for losing control of her animal, she would recommend a muzzle for her dog while in public. Better to have a cow savaged than a child.

"It's not as bad as I thought," she told Ephraim. "I'm going to stitch her up."

He nodded. "Do whatever you can."

Abigail worked quickly. She carefully anesthetized the cow's flank where she intended to suture. Then she rummaged in her duffel bag for sutures and a needle.

It took half an hour of careful stitching to

get the cow sewn up. During that time, crowds wandered in and out, though many stayed to watch. Ephraim remained unmoving by the cow's head, stoically holding the animal's halter and keeping her calm. The woman with the dog stayed on the sideline, hiccuping once in a while, but otherwise not moving. Abigail was barely aware of her surroundings. Her entire focus was on repairing the animal in front of her.

At last Abigail felt satisfied over her handiwork. She gave the cow a shot of antibiotics as a final precaution, then stood back. As often happened when helping an injured animal, she felt a warm glow inside her, a confirmation that her skills were from *Gott* and not something to be taken lightly.

She put her supplies back in the duffel bag and turned to speak to Ephraim. However, the farmer jerked his head toward something behind her, a meaningful expression in his eyes.

Abigail whirled. She had been so involved she hardly considered the ebb and flow of people around her, but now she realized one person had been standing nearby the whole time. A man, obviously a photographer since he was armed with elaborate equipment, had clearly been taking pictures of her as she worked.

She thinned her lips. "May I help you?" she asked.

"Just wondering how an Amish woman can do what you're doing. I thought they sewed quilts, not cows."

She bit back an uncharitable retort and instead quipped, "Don't underestimate us. They're actually quite similar."

She was gratified to see a flare of uncertainty in his eyes before he gave her a vague smile. "Right," he said. He held up his camera. "I hope you don't mind that I photographed you."

Silently she thumbed toward the obvious signage over the booth requesting no photography.

"Oh." Again he looked crestfallen. "Sorry," he muttered.

She relented. "I should explain I'm a licensed veterinarian," she admitted. "I'm just here visiting."

He eyed her *kapp*. "Then you're not Amish?"

She clamped down on a quiver of uncertainty. "I was born and raised Amish."

"I've never met an Amish veterinarian before. Actually, I haven't met any Amish at all." He reached into a pocket and withdrew a business card. "My name is Charles Young. I'm a reporter from Billings. I heard there were

Amish demonstrations here in Pierce and decided it was worth an article. I'd like to interview you, at your convenience."

Abigail took the card and glanced at it. The one overwhelming thought in her mind was the bishop's warning about influencing other church members to pursue a worldly degree. She was also keenly aware that an interview in a newspaper was little more than pride. *Hochmut.* It was an impossible request.

"I'm sorry, Mr. Young." She handed him back his business card. "I prefer not to be interviewed."

He blinked in what seemed like sheer surprise. "Th-that's a first," he stuttered. "Most people would jump at the chance to be in the newspaper."

"You said you've never met any Amish before?" she asked.

"That's right…"

"Then one of the first things you'll learn about us is we don't care for publicity. We agreed to this demonstration—" she waved a hand across the whole area "—merely as Amish appreciation and awareness for the town of Pierce, which is our new home. That's all."

"But—but that's what an interview would

do!" the man argued. "It would help people understand the Amish!"

"Please, Mr. Young, I have a cow to attend to." She reached down and picked up her duffel bag of supplies. "May I direct your attention to our bishop? He can address the issue of an interview. Not me."

"I see." Mr. Young pocketed his card. "Where would I find him?"

"Do you see that booth?" She started to point toward Benjamin's booth, then realized it was empty. Instead, Benjamin was lurking on the edge of the crowd, obviously listening. She nodded toward him. "This gentleman can help you find our bishop."

As if on cue, Benjamin walked forward. *"Ja,* I can. Will you come with me?"

She exhaled a deep breath as Benjamin escorted the reporter away. She turned to Ephraim, who quirked an amused eyebrow at her. "Persistent" was all he said.

"Ja." She looked at the cow. "She'll be fine, Ephraim. She might be off her milk for a day or two, and you might keep her inside the barn tomorrow. I'll be by in about a week to remove the stitches."

"Vielen Dank, Abigail. This could have been so much worse."

"I agree. Meanwhile, I'll go talk to the woman

whose dog attacked. If nothing else, it needs to wear a muzzle. Can I leave my duffel bag here?"

"*Ja*, of course."

Abigail tucked the bag into a corner, then turned to find the dog's owner.

The woman had retreated to a nearby bench and was tightly gripping the leash of the dog, a large German shepherd mix. Her face was ravaged from crying.

As Abigail approached, the woman bounced to her feet, and the dog stood up as well. She began babbling apologies, but Abigail held up a hand to silence her and turned her attention to the dog, letting him sniff her. He took his time doing so, since she had traces of blood on her. But at last he permitted her to stroke his head, and even wagged his tail.

The barrier crossed, Abigail gestured to the woman. "Sit down. We need to talk." She seated herself.

The woman dropped bonelessly onto the bench. "I'll pay for all the vet bills, I can't believe he did that…"

"Ma'am, calm down. What's done is done. It's better that he attacked a cow than a child."

"Oh, he'd never attack a child…"

"But you didn't know he would attack a cow, either."

A look of hysteria crossed the woman's face. "You're not suggesting I have him put down?"

"Of course not! He's a beautiful dog." She stroked the canine's head. "But you must understand, this incident has opened you up to a lawsuit. Oh, not from us, don't worry. But any time a dog attacks, it becomes a liability issue."

"You talk like a vet."

"I *am* a vet. I work out of state and I'm just here visiting. But as a vet, I'll need to report this incident to the authorities. That's why I strongly recommend you have your dog wear a muzzle while out in public from now on. With a legal incident filed against him, a muzzle demonstrates you're taking the issue seriously."

"But I said I'd pay for everything…!"

With a touch of irritation, Abigail waved her hand. "There are no costs. I've taken care of the cow, and she'll be fine. Ma'am, please understand it's not a matter of payment, it's a matter of liability."

She'd met pet owners before who simply could not believe—notwithstanding all evidence in front of their very eyes—that their animal was capable of aggression.

Despite her earlier hysteria, anger and denial flooded the woman's features, and she jerked to her feet. "You can't file anything with the authorities if you don't know who I am," she snapped with a look of triumph. "I'm leaving and there's nothing you can do about it."

She snatched at the dog's leash and disappeared into the crowd.

Abigail heard someone come up behind her, and saw Benjamin. She exhaled in frustration. "No matter how much weeping and wailing she does, she refuses to accept responsibility for her dog's behavior. I hope he doesn't do anything worse. Did you help Mr. Young find the bishop?" she added.

"*Ja*, and happily turned the reporter over to let him deal with it. You handled him well, Abigail. Far better than I would have."

She looked at the ground, feeling a girlish quiver at the rare compliment. *"Danke."* Then she raised her eyes to meet his. "You want to know what was going through my head when he said he wanted an interview? My meeting with the bishop. He warned me about influencing *youngies* to leave and get a worldly degree, and I didn't want to be involved in something that might make that come true."

"That was wise thinking." He glanced around. "I'd better get back to my booth."

"I'll go with you. My work is finished here."

* * *

Benjamin was impressed with how Abigail handled herself with the reporter and the dog owner. But even he had to admit, those two were the low points of an otherwise fun and eventful day.

Jonathan Turnkey came by the booth toward evening. "Well, Benjamin," he boomed. "I'd say this whole day has been a rousing success." He reached over to shake his hand. "I'm sorry you won't be here tomorrow, since the fair runs the whole weekend."

Benjamin shook hands. "It's our Sabbath, of course."

"Right. I understand. Things are usually slower in the morning because most people are in church, but everyone will come pouring in afterward. Your demo area would be very popular."

"I realize that, but the bishop would never approve. Jonathan, have you met Abigail Mast? She grew up in our church back in Indiana. She's here for the summer helping her mother recuperate from surgery."

"Nice to meet you." Jonathan shook Abigail's hand, then turned back to him. "I hope you'll consider repeating this demonstration area next year."

"Well…" He hesitated. "It will be up to our

bishop. I'm not in a position to make unilateral decisions for the community."

"I hope you'll present the idea to him, then." Jonathan glanced over the thinning crowds as the day wound down. "I think this has worked to your church's benefit, though. People are now aware there's an Amish population near Pierce, and that can help your businesses develop."

"*Ja*, no doubt." Benjamin smiled as Jonathan left. Then he let out a sigh and slumped into one of his rocking chairs. "I'm so glad today is over."

"You must be pleased it went so well." She dropped into a chair beside him.

"I am. And I'm over the moon about meeting Greg Anderson. Depending on how many orders he places, I may even have to hire someone to work for me. Plus I received four orders from other visitors."

"Benjamin, that's wonderful!"

He smiled at her. "It makes my future more… secure. It's something that interests me a lot more than it used to."

He saw she understood his unspoken meaning because her face shuttered just a bit. But did he also detect a gleam of longing, or was it his imagination?

"Well." He interrupted his own thoughts

with an attempt at levity. "I'm glad tomorrow is the Sabbath. I intend to fully enjoy my day off."

Her chuckle seemed a bit forced. "You've earned it. Me, I was invited over to Eva's. It's so nice rediscovering her friendship."

"Eva's a *gut* woman," he agreed. "Very well-liked. And," he added, "I have to admit the *Englisch* are much nicer than I anticipated. A little different, *ja*, but Pierce is a nice town full of nice people."

"Sounds like the place is growing on you at last."

He laughed. "I don't know if I'll ever feel totally at ease with the *Englisch*, but I understand I can't hold someone like Jonathan responsible for why Barbara left ten years ago."

"There are many things to admire in the *Englisch* world." Abigail looked out at members of the community as they began the laborious task of breaking down their displays. "But I like it here."

Benjamin didn't respond to that, though his heart leaped. Instead he looked over toward Ephraim King, whose cow Abigail had helped. Ephraim had moved the animal toward the back, away from the spot where the dog had attacked her. The cow looked more comfortable and was chewing her cud.

"I guess we should help everyone pack down," he said. "There is a lot to do to get home before dark."

Chapter Twelve

The next morning, Abigail noted her mother seemed tired. "It was a bit harder than I thought to be away from home all day," Esther admitted. "Even if I didn't do much more than sit in the quilting area."

"And feel like the proverbial fish in a fishbowl," replied Abigail, setting a cup of tea before her.

"*Ja*, very true. But you know what? I think people liked it. I met the nicest *Englisch* lady who asked if she could try her hand at quilting, and she sat next to me for a bit. She's an expert seamstress and always admired quilting, but had never tried it." The older woman's face glowed with pleasure.

"It was interesting, working at the information booth. By the end of the day, my jaw was tired from talking so much. By the way," she added in a teasing tone, "how did you meet this Mark Beiler, the bishop's brother?"

"Oh." Esther flapped a hand, and spots of color formed in her cheeks. "Lois, the bishop's wife, introduced us."

"Any particular reason?"

"*Nein*. She was introducing him to many people."

Abigail didn't push, but it amused her to see her mother blushing. "I'd best be heading for Eva's. I'm stopping at Ephraim King's place on the way to check on his cow."

"Don't forget to bring her some of those pastries—her *kinner* will enjoy them."

"*Ja*, I'll do that."

Abigail packed a basket of pastries amid some vet supplies and set out for Eva Hostetler's farm.

It was a beautiful, quiet summer morning, as befitted the Sabbath. Abigail smelled the fresh mountain air and wondered if she could ever return to her Indianapolis clinic. It was a thought she kept resolutely pushing to the back of her mind. *Gott* had not yet provided her an answer to her dilemma. She was trying to be patient.

First she made a detour to Ephraim's place. She found the older man and his wife seated in rocking chairs on their porch, reading their Bibles.

"Guder mariye!" they called simultaneously when they saw her.

Abigail returned their greeting and stopped at the base of the porch steps. "I'm on my way to visit Eva Hostetler and wanted to see how your cow was doing."

Ephraim rose from his chair. "She is fine, thanks to you. Come and see her."

The cow was lying down and chewing her cud, an excellent sign. Her eyes were calm and alert. She didn't even blink when Abigail looked her over.

"How did she milk this morning?" Abigail asked Ephraim.

"A bit off, as you said she might be, but not bad." He scratched the animal's forehead, and the cow closed her eyes for a moment with enjoyment. "I don't mind keeping her here in the barn for as long as you think it's necessary."

"The wounds are healing nicely. She'll have a bit of scarring, but I'm thankful the damage was to her flank and not her udder. Let me know if you see any change in her condition, including lethargy, but otherwise I think she'll be fine until it's time to remove the stitches."

"Ja, gut."

Abigail left the Kings' farm and continued on the road toward Eva's.

Her old friend sat on the porch with her husband, chatting and sipping lemonade, supervising her two young children playing in the yard. She had started wearing a maternity dress, though her middle was barely thickened. She raised an arm and waved as Abigail approached. *"Guder mariye!"* she called. "You're just in time for lemonade."

"And I've brought some pastries *Mamm* sent," replied Abigail. *"Guder mariye,* Daniel. How are you today?"

Eva's husband was a pleasant-looking man with mild blue eyes and laugh crinkles at the corner of his eyes. His chestnut-brown beard was full, and he had the contented look of a man satisfied with his life.

"I'm fine, *danke.* Glad yesterday is finished, and that today is not a church Sunday." His eyes twinkled. "In fact, if you and Eva would like to visit, I hear a hammock calling my name." He pointed toward some stout netting slung invitingly between two trees.

"Not until you have one of *Mamm*'s pastries." Abigail fished a container out of her bag.

"One of Esther's pastries? You don't have to convince me." Daniel took the delicacy, snatched a napkin off the tray with the lemonade and made his way toward the hammock.

Eva called over her children to take a pastry. The children ate, then dashed back into the yard to play.

Abigail settled into Daniel's chair with a sigh. "*Ach*, yesterday was busy. I'm so glad today is the Sabbath."

Eva chuckled. "I think many people feel that way. I imagine Benjamin is happy it's over and that it went so well."

"I think so, *ja*." Abigail glanced over at her friend. "You look so happy, Eva."

"I am." Eva's gaze rested on the grass, where her children were playing in a sandbox, and where her husband was relaxing in the hammock. "*Gott* has been *gut* to me." Her eyes sharpened. "But what an unusual comment to make out of the blue. Does this mean you're *not* happy?"

"*Nein*, I wouldn't say that. It's just that…" She sighed and left the thought unfinished.

"Are you staying in Montana?" Eva nibbled a pastry.

Abigail felt the full weight of her friend's simple inquiry. "That's the big question." She stared at her glass of lemonade. "I don't know if you heard, but the bishop more or less gave me an ultimatum. I can stay and be baptized, but give up practicing animal medicine. Or I can continue my career but forgo baptism. It's a hard decision, Eva." Without warning, she felt tears prickle her eyes. "I've been trying not to think about it, trying to take direction from *Gott*, but I don't have any clear answers yet."

"So you're in limbo."

"*Ja*, and it's an uncomfortable feeling."

"I can imagine whatever you decide is of prime interest to Benjamin, too."

Startled, Abigail snapped her head up. "What do you mean?"

"It's obvious, isn't it? He wants you to stay."

"*Ja*, but to what end? We have no future, Eva. At least not until I'm settled."

Eva cocked her head. "Is the pull from the *Englisch* world that strong? To leave here and go back to being a vet?"

"*Ja*, at times." Abigail scrubbed a hand over her face. "It's a calling, Eva. That's the only way I can describe it. But why would that put me at odds with the people I grew up with? That's what I don't understand."

"*Mamm! Mamm!*" Eva's little girl, Mildred, came running up. "Did you see the butterfly? It landed right on Jacob's head!"

Eva chuckled at her child's enthusiasm. "Do you think it was *Gott*'s way of giving him a kiss?"

The little girl's eyes grew large. "*Ja!* I'll go tell him!" She dashed down the porch steps and over to her brother.

Abigail followed the child with her eyes. "That's another thing, Eva. The Lord tells us not to covet, but I'm coveting your family. I never thought I'd be in this position, a woman my age with no *kinner*."

"It's not too late, you know. You're no *grossmammi* yet."

"I know…"

"But I must say, the contrast between our different paths in life is remarkable." Eva sipped her lemonade. "I often thought of you out in the *Englisch* world, grappling with your studies. Becoming a veterinarian—that's a lot of book learning. Do you have any regrets?"

"Sometimes." Abigail gestured toward the children. "Like right now. But I can't imagine you have any regrets about the path you've chosen?"

"None." A look of contentment startlingly similar to her husband's crossed Eva's face. "Daniel and I get along so well, like bread and butter. He's everything I could hope for in a *hutband*. I try to be everything he could hope for in a wife."

The simple equation for marital happiness made Abigail blink hard. The benefits of that equation went beyond Eva and Daniel. They extended to the children playing in the yard, and the unborn baby inside Eva. Someday those children would make similar decisions about a spouse, and the blessings would carry on through future generations.

None of this was unfamiliar to Abigail. Her own brothers and sisters were happily settled. Her *mamm* had enjoyed many loving years with her *daed*. It was only she, Abigail, who had stepped off the familiar path into the unknown territory, following a *Gott*-given call toward animal medicine.

But at what price?

She verbalized out loud what Benjamin had asked her weeks ago. "Is this something I can do ten years from now?" she wondered. "Or twenty years from now, when it will be too late to have children?"

Eva looked at her with sympathy in her eyes. "It comes down to how strong the pull is, I suppose," she said. "I've never had a calling like that. I've heard they can be great blessings, but difficult to bear. I just never expected to see that conflict in action, so to speak."

Abigail nodded. "It's funny. Yesterday after I finished sewing up Ephraim's cow, I felt what I often feel after helping an animal—a warm glow inside me. I've always seen that as a confirmation my skills are not something to be taken lightly. Definitely not something that should be put aside. That's the hard part, Eva. The bishop told me I must put aside my gift to become baptized."

Eva winced. "An impossible decision."

"*Ja.* Out in the *Englisch* world, there is great emphasis on women having careers. But that's not what this is for me. Careers can come and go, careers can change, careers can be put aside while concentrating on something else, such as raising a family. But gifts from *Gott*? Those aren't so easy. Sure, I could put it aside, become baptized and never practice medicine again. But could *you* so easily toss a blessing back into the face of *Gott*?"

Eva shook her head. "Sounds to me this is something you need to discuss with the bishop."

"I tried." She remembered her sour conversation with the church leader. "And failed. He's a *gut* man, the bishop, but he has no understanding how strong my calling is, or why it was given to a woman."

Comprehension dawned in Eva's eyes. "I see. If this were Daniel, or even Benjamin, it wouldn't be nearly as complicated, *ja*? But because you're a woman, the bishop can't understand why you simply can't exchange one job for another—why you can't exchange being a vet with being a mother. Is that it?"

"*Ja*, that's it exactly." Abigail felt relieved Eva understood. "But he's right. Let's say for the sake of argument that I got married and had children. How could I continue being a veterinarian under those conditions? Being a mother is a full-time job. I couldn't give the task of raising them to someone else. That's my conflict, Eva. I can't do both things at the same time."

Her friend nodded. "It would take a special kind of *hutband* to understand that conflict."

Abigail's first thought, naturally, was whether Benjamin could be that special kind of *hutband*. But it was immaterial whether or not he could accept a wife with outside commitments. The bishop had already made the church's position clear.

Benjamin paced up and down his porch, watched by a patient Lydia, who was taking a break from her puppies. Occasionally he wiped his sweaty palms on his trousers. He'd seen Abigail walk away and knew she was visiting Eva. He just didn't think she would take so long.

With a sigh of irritation—at himself—he dropped into one of the porch rockers that were his specialty to build. Of all the days he wanted to ask Abigail to be his wife, why did he have to choose a day when she would be off visiting people?

He'd thought about this, prayed about it, agitated about it. He knew it was a risky thing, since Abigail wasn't baptized and still felt conflicted about staying.

But maybe he could convince her.

It was that little issue—convincing her—that worried him. He knew she had feelings for him, but were those feelings strong enough to overcome her commitment to animal medicine?

He was seriously thinking about having a heart-to-heart talk with the bishop in hopes the church leader would loosen his strictures against Abigail's career. But he knew what the older man would say: that one exception would soon turn into multiple exceptions, and before long young people would expect to be able to leave the community, do whatever they want, then return and expect no consequences from their behavior.

He absently stroked Lydia's fur while staring blankly across the lawn in front of his cabin. In his mind's eye, he saw the space filled with children and playthings. He was ready for a family…and he knew the woman he hoped would build that family with him.

But if Abigail would not—or could not—be baptized, he couldn't marry her. It was as simple as that. He had already made a lifelong vow to remain with the church during his own baptism. It was not an option to compromise that vow in the interests of marrying an outsider.

He closed his eyes. Despite his best intentions, he'd done it again. He'd fallen in love with a woman with ties to the *Englisch* world, and he knew he risked losing Abigail to that world.

A noise from Lydia caused him to snap open his eyes. The large Pyrenees dog stood up and wagged her tail, staring through the trees at a solitary figure that walked with a basket in her hands.

Benjamin rose to his feet, wiped his hands down the sides of his trousers once more and walked toward the road to meet her.

"I have some nice fresh lemonade if you'd like to join me," he said with a guileless smile. "We can celebrate the end of the Mountain Days ordeal."

She chuckled, her brown eyes crinkling in the summer sun. "I had lemonade at Eva's, but I wouldn't mind a cup of hot tea if you were to offer."

"It seems a bit warm for hot tea, but it's easily done."

"And how's this darling girl?" Abigail dropped her basket on the ground and kneeled down to fuss over Lydia. "It looks like she's fully recovered. I'm so glad."

"She's taking a break from her puppies." Benjamin paused to admire Abigail's starched *kapp* from above and how it contrasted with the dark hair it covered. "They're getting pretty demanding."

She laughed and rose to her feet as she picked up her basket. "She seems like a *gut* mother."

"She is. Come on in." He turned and made his way to the cabin.

Abigail walked beside him, then stopped for a moment as they approached the house.

He turned. "What's wrong?"

"Nothing." She gestured toward his home. "Just admiring the cabin. I stop and admire it every time I come here. It's just so pretty."

He was surprised and gratified. "*Ja*, I feel blessed to have it. I don't know when it was built, but I'm guessing sometime in the nineteen-forties. It has a venerable feel to it."

"It just sits so well in this landscape." She gazed around at the towering pines, the snow-capped mountains behind, and the cozy log cabin before them. "Sometimes I feel like I've stepped into a postcard. It's so classically Montana, or at least my impressions of Montana long before I ever came here."

It was the perfect opening to inquire if she planned to stay here, but Benjamin chickened out. Instead he let her admire the view a moment or two longer, then reissued his offer of hot tea.

The cabin's interior was typical of any number of Amish households: uncurtained windows, an oil lamp centered on the plain kitchen table, hearty cookstove along one wall, wide pine flooring. The kitchen was contiguous with the living room, which sported a braided rag rug his mother had made him years ago nestled between several comfortable chairs he had collected or made through the years.

Abigail touched the kitchen table. "You made this, I suppose?"

"*Ja*, of course." He filled the kettle and placed it on a propane burner, since the weather was far too warm to use the wood cookstove. "I made most of the furnishings except those easy chairs in there." He pointed toward the living room. "But there were excellent thrift stores in Indiana, so I found some comfortable seating."

"It's nice. Cozy. While the water is heating, I have to fuss over my little boy." She made her way to the closet, where the puppies were sleeping in a pile. She fished out the youngest one and brought him back to the table, where she cuddled him in her lap. "Look, his badger markings are getting darker." She touched the coloration on the puppy's face.

"He's the biggest of the litter so far." Benjamin pulled together the tea things and waited for the kettle to boil. When he poured the water into the mugs, to his annoyance his hand trembled and he spilled some of the water.

Abigail looked at him sharply. "Are you okay?"

"*Ja*, I'm fine." He set down the kettle and pushed her mug across the table.

She lifted the paper tag and dipped the tea bag up and down with one hand while holding the puppy to her chest with the other. "You seem distracted."

"I am." Abruptly he sat down. "I guess I'll just blurt it out. Abigail, I want to court you."

She froze and stared at him. "Benjamin..."

He waved a hand. "I know your concerns. Believe me, Abigail, I know them very well. The whole time you've been here, I've been kicking myself for falling in love with a woman with one foot in the *Englisch* world... again. But it is what it is."

She looked down at the puppy against her chest. "This doesn't come as a surprise, Benjamin. And under any other condition, I'd welcome your courtship."

His heart leaped.

"But that doesn't mean it's wise," she continued. She lifted her head and he saw moisture in her eyes. "It's not that I have one foot in the *Englisch* world, as you put it. It's that I have both feet in the world of animal medicine. You know what the bishop told me. I have to make a choice."

"I'm willing to give you time."

"Time for what? That's not the issue I'm facing. The issue is one of choice. I have to choose which course I want to take."

"But—"

She interrupted, a thread of anger in her voice. "Benjamin, let's say for the sake of argument the bishop allows me to be baptized and still keep my career. If we got married, then children would inevitably follow. Most women in the community don't work outside the home once *bopplin* arrive. It's too difficult to juggle all those responsibilities."

"But—"

She forged ahead again. "Besides, when I was visiting with Eva this morning, she confirmed what I already know—most women in our church consider motherhood the ultimate career. But they don't have the background I do. They didn't spend eight years in school and two years in practice. That's a hard thing to give up." Her eyes filled with tears, and she clutched the puppy closer to her chest.

Something akin to anger settled across him. "Then you're throwing away a chance at love, at happiness, just for the sake of animals?"

"I don't know." Tears spilled over her eyes. She stood up so fast her chair tipped over, and she shoved the puppy at him. "As *Gott* is my witness, *I don't know.*"

She fled. The screen door banged after her.

Benjamin was left with a puppy in his arms. Somehow it seemed symbolic.

Chapter Thirteen

Abigail slept poorly that night. She tossed and turned and thought about the fork in the road ahead of her.

Down one path lay the fulfillment of husband, children, family, church. The thought of marrying Benjamin gave her a deep longing. But despite the domestic draw, somehow it seemed sterile without the single-minded pursuit she had followed for ten years.

Down the other path lay the expression of her gift from *Gott*—animal medicine. That choice was not necessarily incompatible with husband, family or church. But it *was* incompatible with an Amish husband and church ties. Could she face life without Benjamin?

In some ways, life had been so simple before she left the Amish and went to college. She knew the expectations of an Amish woman:

marriage, children, faith. But as a professional veterinarian, those goals became conflicts.

Living back among her community made her realize how much she ached to reembrace the faith ties and connections she'd grown up with. She hadn't realized the depth of that yearning until she had subsumed herself as an adult.

Subsume. That was an accurate word. If she came back to her church roots, she would be expected to follow the *Ordnung*, which meant subsuming her will and her pride to that of the community. It was surprisingly difficult to reconcile herself to that thought.

She dragged herself out of bed early and splashed water on her face, determined to put on a cheerful appearance for her mother. Esther didn't have to know the depth of her despair, or even the offer of courtship from Benjamin—something she knew her mother would welcome. Instead, she started coffee and pulled out ingredients to make muffins for breakfast.

Esther had barely risen and was still in her bathrobe when Abigail heard a knock at the front door.

Instinctively her mother drew the top of her bathrobe closer. "Who could that be so early in the morning?"

"Well, it's not *that* early. You just overslept." Abigail kept her voice light and teasing, but her heart jumped. At this hour, it could only be one person—Benjamin.

But when she opened the door, she was surprised to see a stranger, a middle-aged man with a neat beard and unruly hair, with a sheaf of newspapers tucked under one arm. He was dressed in scrubs.

Scrubs?

Startled, she drew herself up. "Good morning. May I help you?"

The man smiled. He had a pleasant face and cheery blue eyes. "Good morning. I'm sorry to call so early, but I'm trying to find Abigail Mast. Does she live here?"

"I'm Abigail Mast."

He stuck out a hand to shake. "How do you do? I'm Dr. John Green. I own the veterinarian clinic in town."

Automatically she shook hands. "What can I do for you, Dr. Green?"

"Do I understand you're a veterinarian?"

How did he know that? "Er, yes. Yes, I am, though I'm not licensed to practice in Montana."

He smiled wider. "Do you have a few minutes to talk?"

Baffled as to what this could mean, she nodded. "I'd invite you in for a cup of coffee, but my mother just got up. Please excuse me a moment."

She left him standing at the door and went into the kitchen. "It's a man from the vet clinic in town," she hissed at her mother. "He wants to talk to me, I don't know why. I've invited him in for coffee. Why don't you go get dressed?"

Esther, to her credit, didn't argue. She merely limped from the kitchen, through the living room, and closed her bedroom door behind her.

Abigail returned to the front door. "Please come in."

The man followed her into the kitchen and sat in the chair she indicated while she poured him a cup of coffee, then one for herself. She sank down in the chair opposite. "As a matter of interest, Dr. Green, how did you know I'm a vet?"

"Please, call me John. And I knew because of this." He spread out one of the newspapers in front of her.

Abigail glanced down and gasped in surprise. A photo of her was splashed across the front page. Her face wasn't visible, but she was crouched down in front of Ephraim King's cow, suturing the wounds from the dog attack. Her *kapp* was clearly visible, her dress and apron puddled on the ground as she kneeled before the animal.

The caption read, "Amish veterinarian treats cow injured in dog attack at Mountain Days Festival."

She groaned. "I didn't realize he was taking photos at the time. The bishop will *not* be pleased."

Dr. Green looked puzzled. "Why would he not be pleased? It's a charming picture."

Trying to explain to an *Englischer* the complexities behind the Amish stricture on photography—as well as her own tightrope she was walking—seemed futile at the moment. Instead, she changed the subject. "Is there something I can do you for, Dr. Green? I mean, John?"

He sipped his coffee. "You said you weren't licensed in Montana. Where are you licensed?"

"Indiana. I went to school there, graduated two years ago and was working at a clinic in Indianapolis. We handled both large and small animals. Having grown up on a farm, I especially like working with farm animals." She glossed over her experience with the dog she'd nearly lost. "I took a leave of absence since my widowed mother had hip-replacement surgery a couple months ago, so I came here to take care of her while she recuperated. In fact, here she is."

Esther, properly dressed, limped slowly into the kitchen.

Abigail conducted introductions. "Dr. John Green, this is my mother, Esther Mast."

John rose and shook the older woman's hand. "How do you do, ma'am? I'm sorry to call so early, but I wanted to talk with your daughter before I went to work."

"Nice to meet you," replied Esther politely. She looked at Abigail. "I'll take my coffee onto the porch. It's such a beautiful morning." She poured herself a cup and shuffled outside.

John smiled. "That's to give us privacy in our discussion, is that it?"

"Ja." She smiled back. "But she's probably just as bewildered as I am why you're here."

"Then I'll come right to the point. Are you looking for a job?"

If he'd started tap dancing on the kitchen table, Abigail couldn't have been more shocked. She stared at him, speechless.

He continued into the silence, "Rural veterinarians are surprisingly hard to find. One of our older vets wants to retire, and we were going to advertise to find a replacement. I'd like to invite you to apply. Our pay scale will be lower than what you might be making in a comparable clinic in a more urban area, but it's not bad for this region. The clinic will even pay for your Montana certification."

She rubbed her forehead. "This comes as quite a surprise…"

"Evidently." He chuckled. "Did you have immediate plans to return to Indiana?"

"I—I'm drifting a bit at the moment." She sighed and wondered how much to tell him, then decided to be honest. "Dr. Green—John—I don't mean to sound like I'm waffling, and I appreciate your generous offer, but I don't know how to respond yet. In a nutshell, I'm facing a conflict with my church." She plucked at her apron. "I may look Amish, but I'm not baptized. I'm now facing a choice—to leave my church behind and work as a professional, or leave my calling behind and become a fully baptized church member."

To her relief, he did not dismiss the issue as insignificant. He nodded with gravity. "That is quite a conflict. I'm a man of faith myself, so I understand what it's like to stand at a spiritual crossroad. I won't pressure you to make up your mind one way or the other, of course. But in the meantime, why don't you come see our clinic and meet our staff? It's best to be fully informed, as I imagine you know."

"*Ja*, of course. I would like that."

"If you're free right now, I can drive you in, show you around and drive you back. Otherwise you're welcome to come see it at your convenience."

Her professional curiosity was piqued. "Now would be fine. Let me just make sure my mother doesn't need anything."

"I'll wait in my truck while you explain things to her and get her settled." He rose.

Abigail followed him out the front porch. "It was nice meeting you, Mrs. Mast," he said, and walked toward the pickup truck parked a short distance away.

Esther stared after him. "What was all that about?"

Abigail sank into one of the porch chairs. "*Mamm*, he wants to hire me to work in the vet clinic in town."

Esther's eyes widened. "And what did you tell him?"

"The truth—that I can't give him an answer yet. But he offered to show me around the clinic. Will you be okay if I'm gone for an hour or so?"

"*Ja*, sure, I'll be fine." Esther flapped a hand. "I'll be curious to hear all about it. But don't let him bully you into anything you don't want to do, *liebling*."

"He doesn't strike me as the bullying type,

but you're right, *Mamm*. I won't be bullied into anything."

Making sure her *kapp* was neatly in place, she walked toward the pickup truck.

"It's been quite a while since I've driven in a motor vehicle," she ventured as he put the truck in gear and set off down the gravel road.

"Those of us in town have watched with interest as the Amish church settled here," he said. "I haven't talked to anyone yet who hasn't thought you've all been fine additions to the community."

"That's *gut*. Good. That's why our bishop agreed to have the church members participate in the Mountain Days event on Saturday. He wanted to make sure we are cooperative with the people in town."

"I was at the event but missed the whole incident with the dog attacking the cow. It's a good thing you were nearby and had some medical supplies with you."

"A lot of our church members have turned to me to help with their animals since I've been back," she admitted. "I can't take any payment, of course, but I've started an ad hoc clinic in a shed a neighbor helped retrofit. However, I can't do much, since it lacks both electricity and modern equipment, such as an X-ray machine."

"We're fully equipped," he replied. "I started the clinic about twenty years ago, specializing in large-animal work. There used to be a second clinic in town, mostly concentrating on small-animal work, but the vet who ran it retired, so we inherited his customer base. We brought in two of his vets, so now we offer a full range of services for both farms and small animals. We employ four vets, two vet techs and the clerical staff. We're a close-knit group."

"Sounds lovely." She hesitated. "The clinic where I worked could be tense at times. The head vet was brilliant, but he had a volatile temper. We felt we were walking on eggshells a lot of the time."

He smiled. "We're nothing like that, but I know just the type you mean. There's a lot of ego and insecurity tied up in people who behave that way."

His simple explanation sent a shaft of understanding through Abigail. She thought back to Robert and finally recognized that, for all his brilliance, he was likely covering up a certain amount of personal self-doubt. "Interesting," she murmured.

"Here we are." John pulled up behind the modest clinic and unbuckled his seat belt. He paused and smiled at her. "I'd like to say 'welcome'…but I'll understand if that's premature. Meanwhile, let me introduce you around."

Abigail followed him into the building.

Benjamin vaguely noticed a pickup truck come and go from Esther's cabin, but he was too distracted to give it much thought. Instead, he worked on formulating his case to present to the bishop. Abigail had no idea, but he planned to plead with the church leader on her behalf.

The day promised to be hot as he set off toward Bishop Beiler's home. Back in Indiana, the bishop and his wife lived in a *daadi haus* behind their youngest son's farmhouse. Here, however, the community had renovated an old barn into a cozy little home set well off the gravel road. Lois Beiler kept a garden and chickens, and the bishop limited himself to raising a few pigs for the table.

He found them in the garden, wearing oversize straw hats and harvesting peas. Benjamin waded in amid the flourishing vegetables. "*Guder mariye*, both of you."

They looked up. The bishop straightened and exclaimed, "Benjamin! *Welkom*. What can we do for you?"

Benjamin resisted the urge to wipe sweaty palms on his trousers. "I wonder if I could speak to you for a few minutes, Bishop?"

The older man looked at him for a moment without speaking. Then he turned to his wife. "Not too long in the sun, okay, *geliebte*?"

Lois smiled. "*Ja.* There's some lemonade in the icebox if you'd like to sit on the porch."

"*Danke.*" Carrying his basket of pea pods, the bishop inclined his head toward Benjamin. "Shall we get something cool to drink? It's warm out here."

"*Ja, danke.*"

Within a few minutes, Benjamin found himself seated opposite a small table in a comfortable rocking chair, with a glass of lemonade before him. A handsome calico cat with stunning green eyes promptly jumped onto the bishop's lap and curled his head beneath the older man's chin. The bishop chuckled and stroked the animal. "This is Thomasina, my favorite pet," he explained. "I'd be lost without her."

"I can tell." Benjamin sipped his drink, more out of nervousness than thirst.

The bishop regarded him with mild eyes. "You're as nervous as a cat, Benjamin."

"*Ja.* Maybe I am. I'm here to ask a difficult question."

"I'll do my best to answer."

"Bishop... I want to court Abigail Mast. But I can't, since she's not baptized. She said she had a conversation with you some time ago about the choice she had to make—to stay or to go. To remain a veterinarian or to be baptized. She's wrestled with it ever since."

Bishop Beiler nodded and leaned back. The cat curled up in his lap, and he absently stroked the animal's fur. "I understand your hesitation. I also believe I understand Abigail's confusion. But, Benjamin, did she tell you my concerns?"

"*Ja.* Basically, she must choose one of two options."

"That is correct. I do not believe those two options are compatible. I'm glad to hear she understood what I was trying tell her."

"But surely you don't think she would ever try to influence anyone to leave the church?"

"Have you seen the newspaper this morning?"

Baffled at the abrupt change of topic, Benjamin stared for a moment. *"Nein."*

"Since I have a cat on my lap, I'll ask if you can step inside the house and fetch the newspaper on the kitchen table."

Puzzled, Benjamin did as he was asked, bringing the folded-up paper back outside to the porch.

"Take a look at the front page," urged the bishop.

Benjamin unfolded the paper and saw a huge

photograph of Abigail as she was working on the injured cow on Saturday.

"Oh, no…" he breathed, and dropped back into the rocking chair.

"As you can imagine, this didn't please me," said the bishop.

"But surely you know she had nothing to do with it?"

"Of course she didn't. But still, her photo is in the newspaper for all to see."

"But I overheard her conversation with the photographer that day," Benjamin argued. "She said she wasn't interested in any publicity and refused to be interviewed. She pointed out the signage requesting no photography. She's not responsible because some *Englischer* paid no attention."

"Regardless of how it happened, the fact remains. Her photo is in the paper. This tells other young people in our church about a glamorous possibility—that they can behave in a manner contrary to the *Ordnung*, and get rewarded for it. It smacks of *hochmut*. Pride."

Benjamin felt a sliver of annoyance run through him at the bishop's stubbornness. "Are you suggesting she should have stood by and done nothing when Ephraim's cow was attacked? The animal might have died."

"Not at all. She did the right thing. It was

her choice to become a veterinarian, and she's obviously *gut* at what she does. But in making that choice, she left the church."

"Did she tell you *why* she became a veterinarian?"

The bishop waved a hand. "Something about how a vet saved one of her favorite cows when she was a child."

"It goes deeper than that. Far, far deeper. She knew the ramifications of what would happen when she left to go to school, but she went anyway—because she was called by *Gott* to study animal medicine. Each of us must follow the path *Gott* lays out before us. To stray from that path can only lead to being separated from *Gott*. Abigail desperately wants to be baptized, but she cannot lay aside the gift she was given in order to do so. Can you have no clemency toward that conflict?"

"Benjamin, I've made my position clear. Abigail knows she has to make a decision, and I won't blame her for whatever choice she makes. But she cannot have it both ways."

Abruptly, Benjamin stood up. "I'm sorry to find you so resolute. You're putting her in a difficult position."

The bishop raised his chin and looked stern and sad at the same time. "Benjamin, I don't want any bad blood between us. You're a *gut* solid member of the church, and I value your counsel. Can you not see things from my perspective? I am not a dictator. I was given the role of bishop by lot—chosen by *Gott*'s hand. I have to consider the needs of the entire community, not just the needs of a single person who chose to step outside that community to develop her gift. Now let me ask you something," he added. "Did Abigail send you here to talk to me?"

His anger faded and he sat back down, bowing his head. "*Nein*, I came here of my own volition. I asked her yesterday if I could court her. She said no, because she wasn't baptized. It's—it's like *Gott* keeps taking away the women I love, Bishop. I didn't mean to fall in love with Abigail, but it seems I have."

"At least she's aware of the barriers," said the bishop. "Despite her choice to leave us for an education, she's grown into a steady, solid young woman and a contributing member of the community."

"But you're not willing to relent on the last step she would need to take?"

"It's not in my hands, Benjamin." The bishop's voice was firm. "The decision is in her hands."

Chapter Fourteen

The Pierce Veterinary Clinic was a bright and cheerful place. Framed prints of Montana's spectacular scenery decorated the walls of the waiting room and examination rooms. Behind the receptionist's desk was a wall of client files. John Green walked her through the facility's amenities: the kennels out back, the small animal cages inside, the surgery, the X-ray machine, the paddocks in back with holding facilities for horses and cows. Her eyes sparkled at the thought of practicing here.

"It'll be quiet in here today because Mondays are usually our farm-call or house-call days," explained John. "We don't schedule in-clinic appointments. Most of us are in and out of the office on Mondays. Generally we have a vet on call for walk-ins, but even then it's not unusual to be without a vet in the office.

Even our small-animal vet does house calls on Mondays. Ah, here comes Steve." Walking her around the horse paddock, John pointed to an incoming pickup truck. "That's Steve Morrison, our vet who wants to retire. Oh, and here's Lucy Gonzales. She's our small-animal expert. Come and meet them."

By the time the clinic opened its front doors, Abigail had met everyone with the exception of the on-call vet, who worked weekends and was off on Mondays and Tuesdays. She was shown the inventory of medicines, supplies and equipment. She was even given a fast tutorial of the billing system by Cara, the receptionist.

Then John Green drove her home. "I won't ask for a decision right away," he told her. "Steve wants to retire at some point, but he's not in a big rush. However, it's clear you'd fit into the clinic very well. If you have a CV, I'd love to see it, but don't feel the need to give us an immediate answer."

Abigail promised to send him her *curriculum vitae*, as her professional résumé was termed. "I'll keep you posted as to what my decision will be, but as you've gathered, I have a lot to think over."

"I understand." He pulled into Benjamin's driveway, then drove toward Esther's cabin in back. "I apologize for the unorthodox job interview, but it was a pleasure to meet you."

"Likewise." She shook his hand. "I appreciate the vote of confidence." She unstrapped her seat belt, exited the vehicle and watched him drive away.

She felt a tumultuous volcano inside her. Her professional interests warred with her spiritual needs.

She lifted her eyes skyward. "Any other surprises in store for me, *Gott*?" she murmured. It seemed almost a cruel joke to have such a job offer laid at her feet at a time when she was being tugged in so many directions already. She scrubbed a hand over her face and went inside to find her mother knitting in the living room.

Abigail collapsed onto a sofa. "Whew."

"Well…?" prompted her mother after a short silence.

"It's perfect," pronounced Abigail in the gloomiest voice possible. "The facility is clean and modern, the staff is lovely, the clientele includes a lot of farm calls and the pay is generous for this area. In short, I could be very happy there."

"Except for one thing," her mother added.

"Except for the matter of whether or not to be baptized." She covered her face with her hands. "As *Gott* is my witness, *Mamm*, I don't know what to do."

"Ach, liebling." Her mother lurched to her feet and dropped down onto the sofa next to her. Abigail leaned into her mother's shoulder and burst into tears. For a little while she was a child again, drawing comfort from a mother who had stood firm for her daughter as she faced endless difficult decisions in her life.

When the storm passed, Abigail straightened up and mopped her face with a handkerchief. Esther angled herself on the sofa to face Abigail. "I know this is difficult for you."

"It's worse than you think." Abigail twisted the fabric in her hands. *"Mamm*, you should know this. Benjamin waylaid me yesterday on my way back home from visiting Eva. He—he said he wants to court me."

She saw the flare of joy in her mother's eyes. "I didn't know that," Esther murmured.

"But he also said he knew he couldn't," continued Abigail, "because of my status in the church."

"Putting aside the obvious barriers," asked Esther, "is courtship from Benjamin something you would welcome?"

"Ja," she confessed. "It would be." She wiped her eyes with the handkerchief. "Finding someone like Benjamin is the last thing I

expected when I came here to take care of you, but that's what happened. If I took the job in the clinic, it would mean I'm still not a church member, but I would still be near Benjamin. I'm not sure my heart could handle that."

"You might have to move to town to avoid him…"

"*Ja*, I might." She dropped her head in her hands. "In some ways, I wish Benjamin hadn't said anything. It's made my situation even worse. I'm being pushed to stay, to give up my education and be baptized."

"But Benjamin's interest makes things more complicated?"

"*Ja*. It's not just Benjamin, it's a deeper longing. It's funny, *Mamm*. Yesterday when I was visiting with Eva, I couldn't help but notice how happy she was. Her husband is a *gut* man, her children are darling and she's expecting another *boppli*. She's a very content woman. But what do I have? I have a career I've spent ten years developing. But at what cost? If I go back to Indiana, I'll be alone. I won't have a *hutband*, I won't have children, I won't have a church."

Esther made a helpless gesture. "I can't guide you, *liebling*. I see your conflict, but since I've only experienced one side of it, I cannot advise as to the other. I never wanted anything but marriage and children."

"I know. This is my own battle. But maybe what I can't understand is why *Gott* gave me such incompatible longings. I wanted to study animal medicine since I was eight years old. But I love children. I want a family. I want to become baptized. I cannot have it both ways. That's what the bishop told me, and it's true."

"Abigail, let me ask you a serious question." Esther's calm voice pierced her confusion. "What if…? What if you gave up your career and joined the church? What if you gave up your career and married Benjamin? You'd still have your knowledge and skills. You may not be able to practice in a professional setting like the clinic in town, but you could do things informally, kind of like what you've been doing since you arrived. Could you live with that?"

Abigail took a deep breath and stared at the opposite wall. "I don't know," she finally said. "That may be what I'll have to do. There's too much here to give up and return to Indiana. I'd have the church. And I'd have Benjamin."

"And you'd have a very happy mother," added Esther with a small smile. "It's been nice having you home, *liebling*. I'm hopeful the success of the church here in Pierce will convince some of your brothers and sisters to move here, too. I miss being close to my grand-children."

"*Gut*, more pressure," Abigail teased, but it was true. It would be hard to give up the warm and loving relationship she had rediscovered with her mother.

Most Amish young women didn't have to sever ties with their parents. They remained in close contact. When the normal milestones in life came along—courtship, marriage, babies, child-raising—the parents were there to offer guidance and advice.

But Abigail had left her parents behind when she'd reached eighteen and had entered a world her family could not and would not follow. She had missed the parental guidance that kept many young adults from blundering into mistakes. She had avoided committing too many errors in her personal life—aside from her ill-advised interest in Robert—but being around her *mamm* made her realize just how much her mother meant to her, especially since her father had passed away.

It was yet another tie she would miss if she returned to Indiana.

Benjamin sanded a chair leg smooth. His hands worked expertly, but his mind was miles away. He had received an enthusiastic follow-up letter from Greg Anderson, discussing prices and the quantity of furniture he wanted. In many ways, Benjamin's financial future was more secure than it had ever been. But the same couldn't be said for his romantic future.

He kicked himself for baring his soul to Abigail yesterday. He should have known better than to reveal his vulnerabilities.

And now the bishop knew how things stood between them. Why couldn't he have kept his mouth shut?

He thought about Barbara, the young woman he'd courted when he was eighteen. Would he have been happy with her? In retrospect, Barbara had always been somewhat flighty and light-minded. Bound within the vows of matrimony, they would have made a marriage work, of course. But now, for the first time, he felt relief that he hadn't married her.

Or perhaps that conclusion was easy to make when comparing a youthful Barbara to a mature Abigail.

One thing was certain—he didn't think he'd ever met someone as fascinating as Abigail Mast. For such a small woman—no more than two inches over five feet—she packed an astounding amount of skills, abilities, personality and intelligence into a lovely form.

As for the bishop...well, it was perhaps sinful to think dark thoughts about the church leader, but he didn't understand the older man's unaccountable stubbornness over Abigail's future. The only mark against her—even the bishop admitted this—was the conflict of her professional abilities. He insisted she had to pick one or the other—being a vet or being baptized.

Benjamin paused in his work and frowned. For the first time, he looked into the future and tried to imagine Abigail as his wife. For the sake of argument, he pretended the bishop had given permission for her to remain a working veterinarian as well as a baptized member of the church.

That would mean his wife would be working away from home, in an office setting.

Certainly there were many precedents for Amish women working. The Yoders' store in town was proof enough of that. It seemed the only objection the bishop had was Abigail's choice of profession, which had required her to get schooling in the *Englisch* world. But she had chosen to come back to the church.

If that was the bishop's sole concern—that Abigail's decisions might influence other *youngies* to follow her path—then it might be argued she was a *good* example, not a bad one.

But putting that aside, what would married

life be like with a working professional? What would happen when the babies came?

He frowned and resumed sanding. It was all a moot point, anyway. The bishop had not relented, and Abigail had not changed her mind. And once again, Benjamin had fixated his affection on a woman being pulled away from the community.

And yet…and yet, he realized he no longer blamed the *Englisch* for pulling away Barbara or his sister. Nor could he blame them if Abigail chose to leave. The bishop's assignment of putting him in charge of the Mountain Days demonstrations had accomplished that much, at least.

In a moment of insight, he realized his resentment had originated in himself. Deep down he always wondered if something he had said or done had chased away Barbara or his sister. It was easier to pin the blame on the nameless, faceless wider world than to examine his own behavior.

Now that he was older, he realized he was not responsible for the decisions made by his sister, or by Barbara. Nor was he responsible if Abigail chose to leave and go back to the *Englisch* world.

He finished sanding the chair legs and noticed the mail truck just pulling away from his mailbox on the road. Ready for a break from his dark thoughts, he walked the length of the driveway to see what had come in the mail.

Two bills, a letter from his sister Miriam— he smiled at the coincidence—and several pieces of mail for Esther. He would give the older woman her letters when he next saw her.

He frowned at the mail and thought for a few moments, then went inside and checked on Lydia and the puppies. The enormous white dog was lying inside the closet with her puppies heaped in a pile beside her. She wagged her tail when he approached. He crouched down to stroke her fur, then picked up the male puppy whose life Abigail had saved. He stood up, holding the fuzzy baby to his chest. He left the house with the puppy in his arms and the letters in his pocket.

He found Abigail on her porch, rocking slowly in a rocking chair, staring across the landscape. He found it peculiar…and worrisome.

"Abigail?" he ventured.

"What?" She snapped her head around, then pressed a hand to her chest. "I'm sorry, I didn't hear you coming."

"I brought mail for your *mamm*, and a peace offering for you." He climbed the porch steps and deposited the puppy in her lap. "Sometimes it just helps to have an animal to cuddle, *ja*?"

"Oh, Benjamin…" He saw tears start to form in her eyes as she clutched the warm bundle. She buried her face in the animal's fur. "I'm so mixed up…"

He sank down in the nearby rocker, feeling shame for adding to her confusion. "I shouldn't have spoken when I did," he said. "I made the situation worse."

"You're not the only one who has made the situation worse." She fished a handkerchief out of her apron pocket and mopped her face with one hand while clutching the puppy in the other. "I—I… Let me explain," she added. "You probably don't know about my visitor this morning."

"What visitor?"

"Actually, I'll back up a bit further. Did you know the newspaper posted a photo of me sewing up Ephraim's cow at the Mountain Days demo?"

"*Ja*, I saw it," he admitted, hoping she wouldn't ask where. He didn't want to mention his conversation with the bishop this morning.

"Well, the head veterinarian at the clinic in Pierce saw it, too. He stopped by this morning and offered me a job." She wiped her eyes again. "I'm just so torn, Benjamin. Every professional instinct in me says I should accept the position. But everything else says I shouldn't—that I should give up veterinarian work and settle in among the Amish community here." He saw fresh tears start to well up in her eyes. "I've never been so pulled apart in my life, not even when I first left home to go to school."

"And in some ways, there's the one person standing between you and your future." With some bitterness, Benjamin pointed toward the bishop's buggy as the church leader's horse clip-clopped with speed down the road. "Why doesn't he…"

He bit off his words and stared. The bishop's buggy wasn't just passing by. It made a fast turn down his driveway, past his cabin and straight up to Esther's house. The bishop, his face drawn and tense, pulled the panting horse to a stop.

Benjamin sprang to his feet. So did Abigail, clutching the puppy to her chest.

"Abigail, can you help?" croaked the bishop. "My cat was attacked by a coyote."

Abigail shoved the puppy at Benjamin and dashed toward the buggy, where a basket was nestled on the seat. She lifted a blanket and he saw her wince.

She whirled. "Benjamin, tell *Mamm* I'll be

in town at the vet clinic." She climbed uninvited into the bishop's buggy, took the basket on her lap and ordered, "Get going. There's no time to lose."

The bishop wheeled the horse around and took off at a fast trot. Benjamin watched them disappear in a cloud of dust.

Chapter Fifteen

"Tell me what happened." Abigail rested her hand lightly on the blanket and felt the bloodied animal still breathing, making tiny sounds of pain. She said a prayer the cat would make it.

"A coyote came out of the forest near the barn." The bishop's words were clipped, and he concentrated on guiding his horse as quickly as possible along the increasingly busy road toward Pierce. She sensed his emotions were under tight control. "I didn't know the cat was outside until the coyote made a dash and grabbed it. I ran at them with a shovel and actually managed to beat it off, but—but she was so badly mauled." His voice caught. "I don't think I'll ever forget the noise."

Abigail knew how haunting the screams of a cat fighting for its life could be. She also remembered how fond the older man was of this particular animal. "I should warn you, I don't know how much I can do," she admitted. "But with *Gott*'s help, I'll do my best."

The older man swiped his cheek, and she discreetly ignored the sign of his grief. "I have no other option," he stated. "I was hoping you could handle this at your little clinic…"

"I'm limited in what I can do there," she told him. "Proper veterinary care involves equipment I don't have. I can't do surgery there, and I have a feeling that's what will be needed."

Faster than she thought possible, the bishop pulled up to the clinic. "I'll take the cat in," she told him. "You hitch up the horse. I don't want to waste any time."

"*Ja*, go. Go."

He held the basket while she climbed down from the buggy, then handed it down. She burst into the clinic.

Cara, the receptionist, looked up startled. "Abigail! Hello…"

"Sorry to barge in, but I have an emergency. Is the surgery room free?"

"Yes." To her credit, the receptionist didn't argue. Instead she dashed from behind her desk. "Dog or cat?"

"Cat. Mauled by a coyote." Abigail strode into the darkened operating room while Cara followed and flipped on the lights. "The owner is right behind me, attending to his horse and buggy. Is Lucy available?" Abigail had met and liked the small-animal expert.

"No, she's out on a call. All the vets are, in fact. Dr. Green should be back in an hour. But one of the techs is here. Shall I get him?"

"*Ja*, please."

Abigail placed the basket on the counter in the surgery and lifted off the blanket, fearing the cat had already died. But it was still alive. Bloodied and torn, it was making the same pathetic catches of pain in its breath.

She weighed the animal, then immediately sedated it. If nothing else, it was a merciful act to put the animal out of pain while preparing it for whatever repairs were needed.

Thomas LaGrande, the vet tech, bustled in and peered at the animal. "Poor thing," he murmured, then turned to scrub his hands.

"Let's hope she makes it." Abigail closed her eyes and breathed another prayer. It wasn't even so much for the ravaged animal in front of her as it was for the impression she might make on the man out in the waiting room. She prayed for skill—for the skill *Gott* had given her to save injured animals.

For a tense hour, she and Thomas labored over the cat. Abigail started an intravenous drip of saline and antibiotics. Thomas constantly monitored vital statistics. The best surprise was the animal's internal organs appeared undamaged. But the coyote had left some serious bite wounds around the cat's neck, and one of her back legs was shockingly mangled.

"Can you save the leg?" asked Thomas, as the extent of the damage became clear.

Abigail gently probed the injured limb. "I think so. See? The tendon is intact." She pointed. "If the tendon still works, that's half the battle. It seems it's mostly muscular damage we have to deal with. And, of course, the broken femur."

She bent over the operating table, suturing the muscles. Her back cramped and she had to stop and stretch it out once or twice before resuming work.

"You've a good touch with stitches," observed Thomas. "As good as Lucy."

The tech's compliment helped ease the tension. Abigail gave a grim chuckle. "Thank you. I was always good at sewing and quilting when I was a child, and I like to think that early training helped when it came to sewing animals back together."

She was nearly finished repairing the lacerations in the cat's neck when John Green came in. "Cara said you brought in an emergency case. What's the status?"

Abigail finished the last knot and reached for some antibiotic powder, which she dusted liberally over the wounds. "Just finishing up. I think she'll make it." She gave a breath of relief. "It was touch and go for a while. This animal belongs to our church bishop. She's his favorite pet. No pressure there," she concluded with a hint of sarcasm.

John leaned close and examined the wounds Abigail had stitched, and the cast now over the animal's back leg. He listened to her breathing, and gently pried open an eyelid to peer at the ocular membrane. "Well, this is better than any résumé," he said. "Excellent work, Abigail. Her vitals look good and I think she'll make it."

She smiled in pure relief. *"Danke, Gott,"* she breathed to herself. She stripped off her gloves and watched as Thomas gently transferred the cat to a recovery cage. "I'll go talk to the bishop and explain the situation to him."

"Do you want me to come, too?"

"No, but thank you. I'll handle it."

She wiped a hand over her face, took a deep breath and walked out of the surgery room into the waiting area.

The bishop was hunched over in one of the chairs, his head in his hands as if he was in utter despair. Abigail walked quietly toward him. "Bishop?"

He jerked up his head and she saw moisture on his cheeks. He drew a ragged breath. "She's gone, isn't she?"

Her throat closed up at the man's obvious grief. "*Nein*. She's in bad shape, but she didn't have any damage to her internal organs. Her back leg needed a lot of work, so I cleaned it up and set it in a cast. She has some bad bite wounds around her neck, but they're cleaned and sutured now. If animals come through surgery of this scope successfully, their chances of recovery are high."

He stared at her as if he didn't believe her. Then he leaned back, covered his face with his hands and took a shuddering breath.

Abigail had witnessed the agony of people losing a beloved pet many times in her career. Here was the almost agonizing relief of reprieve.

She crouched down before the church leader and briefly touched him on the knee. "You did the right thing bringing her to me immediately. Thanks to your quick thinking and fast response, she's likely to survive."

"No, Abigail." Bishop Beiler removed his hands from his face and looked at her with reddened eyes. "It's thanks to *you* that she's likely to survive. I know it's unworthy to put so much earthly store on a pet, but I raised her from a tiny kitten and I've always loved her. I'm grateful beyond words we'll have more years with her."

"She'll have to stay here a few days," Abigail warned as she stood up.

"You're a mess," the bishop observed with wry humor.

Startled, Abigail looked down at herself. Her apron and dress were indeed a mess—covered with blood, antibiotic ointment and clotting powder. She grunted. "Normally I wear scrubs. I didn't even think about what I was wearing when I took the cat into surgery."

"*Ja*, I meant to ask. How did you—"

He was interrupted when Dr. Green came into the waiting room. "Are you the bishop for the Amish church? I'm Dr. John Green."

"*Ja*. I'm Samuel Beiler." The older man stood up and shook hands. "Did you help with my cat, too?"

"No, I was out on a call. It's all thanks to Abigail's skill that it seems your pet is likely to make it. But we'll have to keep her here for a few days to monitor her recovery."

"*Ja*, sure, that's fine." The bishop fished a handkerchief out of his pocket and mopped his face. "I'm sorry to be so emotional, but she's a *gut* cat. It was hard to see her attacked."

"Coyote?"

"*Ja.*"

The older vet nodded. "They're a serious concern around here."

"My mother's landlord, Benjamin Troyer, raises Great Pyrenees dogs," volunteered Abigail. "I have a feeling they're going to be even more popular after this."

"With good reason," agreed John. "Those dogs are excellent at guarding both livestock and house pets. People, too. We had a fine Pyrenees as a house dog when our children were young, and he would have died to protect our kids from any harm."

"I wonder…" Bishop Beiler hesitated. "Can I see her?"

Abigail frowned. "Your cat?"

"*Ja.*"

"Why would you want to? She's sedated, and frankly she's not a pretty sight at the moment."

"I want to see what you've done." His voice was gentle.

She glanced at John, and he gave a small nod. She sighed. "Then follow me."

She led the way to the animal's recovery cage, where the sleeping cat was lying on a soft blanket. Abigail opened the cage so he could get a better look.

"Don't touch her right now," she advised.

The bishop peered closely at his pet and

swallowed hard. "Tell me what you had to do," he said. "Tell me what wounds she had."

A strange request, but Abigail accommodated him. He stared at his cat for a long time. Then he straightened up and shook his head. "Unbelievable. Miraculous."

"A gift from *Gott*," she murmured.

He shot her a look. "I think I understand that now."

Abigail closed the cage door and led the way back to the waiting room. "We should probably go back now." She was anxious to get home and change clothes. "John, we'll figure out the costs involved in the emergency surgery at a later time." She didn't want him to think she was taking advantage of the clinic's resources without compensation.

The older man nodded. "Most of the expenses are the vet's time and skills," he reminded her. "You're freelance on this."

She nodded. "Thank you."

"How long will the cat have to stay here at the clinic?" asked the bishop.

John looked at Abigail. "It's your patient," he prompted.

"I'm guessing a week," she told the church leader. "I recommend keeping her sedated for at least the next twenty-four hours, and then she'll be on pain medication for several days while recovering from the trauma. After that it's a matter of making sure no infection takes hold. When that danger is over, she can go home. She'll be in that cast for about eight weeks, so her mobility will be impaired."

"And I promise to keep her indoors," added the bishop with a small smile. "Or maybe I should get a Great Pyrenees from Benjamin."

"Ja, gut." She smiled back. It seemed, somehow, that the bishop had turned a corner in his attitude toward her. "Are you ready to go?"

"Ja." Still looking a bit dazed at the events of the last hour, the church leader nodded to John and shuffled out the clinic's glass front door.

John clapped her on the shoulder. "That was some excellent work, Abigail. You're just the kind of vet we're looking for. Please, give some serious consideration to our offer."

"I will, thank you." She looked out the glass doors at the older man unhitching his horse. "He's the one who holds my future in his hands. Maybe it was *Gott*'s will that this all happened."

"Keep me posted." The older vet smiled.

Abigail walked out of the clinic to where the bishop was unhitching his horse. She climbed into the buggy seat. After the church leader had directed the horse out of town, he glanced at her. "I have much to thank you for, but one thing puzzles me. How is it you were able to barge in and conduct surgery in the animal clinic? How is it they know you?"

So much had happened in just the last few hours, it was hard to grasp everything. The bishop didn't know about her unexpected job interview this morning. "Let me tell you about my day," she began.

After Abigail had departed with the bishop, Benjamin visited with Esther for a time while she cooed and fussed over the fuzzy puppy. Then he returned home, nestled the puppy in with his littermates and gave Lydia a pat on the head. He wondered what was transpiring in town. Just this morning he had watched the bishop's display of affection for his cat. Now the poor animal was likely to die. It was a harsh lesson on the ephemeral nature of life.

Restless, he wandered outside, toward the pasture where his cows were chewing their cud under the shade of the fir trees. Elijah, Lydia's mate, was also lying in the shade. His massive head rested on his paws, but his eyes were alert. Benjamin knew he owed his herd's security to the magnificent working dog in the field. It wasn't just coyotes that could stalk livestock. Here in the wilds of western Montana, Benjamin had seen a few wolves, several bears and even a cougar. But thanks to his Great Pyrenees, his cows were safe.

Yes, every last one of Lydia's puppies would be in high demand. But he wanted to hold one back—the youngest pup that Abigail had saved. If only...

Suddenly he heard horse's hooves clopping down the gravel road. The bishop, with Abigail at his side, was directing the buggy down Benjamin's driveway. He walked toward the cabin to meet them.

By the expression on the bishop's face, he suspected Abigail had managed to save the cat, but he waited until the church leader had pulled the buggy to a halt before asking. He walked up to assist Abigail from the buggy. "The cat is likely to make it," she told him.

He smiled in relief. "Praise *Gott*!" Then he noticed her appearance. "You're a mess," he observed.

She laughed. "*Ja*, Bishop Beiler said the same thing. I simply forgot I wasn't wearing scrubs and got right to work."

"And she saved my cat." The bishop finished tying his horse to a post and turned to face them. "Abigail, Benjamin, I want to talk with you both. Is now a *gut* time?"

Benjamin was surprised, and he noticed Abigail seemed equally so. *"Ja,"* he replied with some caution. What on earth did the bishop have to say to them? "I have some lemonade in the icebox. Why don't we sit on the porch, where it's cool?"

"Danke." Somewhat stiffly, the older man walked toward the cabin.

Benjamin caught Abigail's eye and lifted his eyebrows in question. She shrugged her shoulders and shook her head, then followed the bishop toward the porch.

Lydia emerged from inside the house. The giant white dog wagged her tail at the sight of visitors. After greeting everyone, she curled up on the edge of the porch, facing toward the pasture, alert as always for any threats that might be detected.

Benjamin went inside to fetch glasses and a pitcher of lemonade, and came back to see Abigail sitting awkwardly across the small porch table from the church leader. He poured the drinks, then sank into a chair. "Is something the matter, Bishop?"

"Nein. Actually, *ja."* If possible, the church leader looked ashamed. "I owe you an apology, Abigail."

He saw her eyes widen. "For what?"

"For judging you so harshly." The older man clasped and unclasped his hands. "I had it in my head that because you have your degree in animal medicine, you were ineligible to join the church. When Benjamin pleaded your case this morning, I remained inflexible."

Benjamin watched Abigail's head snap around to stare at him. "You pleaded my…"

"*Ja*, he pleaded your case," the bishop said with a small smile. "And I wouldn't budge from my position. I was stubborn…and, dare I say it, perhaps *hochmut*. Then my cat was nearly killed and you saved her life. That changed things. Not because you saved my cat," he added, "but because I had a revelation in the waiting room while wondering if I'd ever see my favorite pet again."

"What kind of revelation?" Benjamin kept his voice soft.

"That pride can affect anyone and everyone. There's a reason the Bible warns against it. I was too proud to admit I was wrong, Abigail. You once told me your skill in veterinary medicine was a gift from *Gott*. I didn't believe you. Or rather, I brushed it aside as unimportant. I've been forcing you to make a harsh decision, to choose between your desire to practice your gift and your desire to join the church."

"And now…?"

"Now I understand what you were saying. Your skills are indeed a gift from *Gott*. The

Bible tells us we're one body in our faith, but we each have different gifts according to the grace given to us. That's why I wanted to see Thomasina while in recovery. *Gott* gave you the skill to save her life. Who am I to deny that?"

Abigail's chocolate-brown eyes welled with tears, but she kept them in check. "D-does that mean you'll allow me to be baptized?"

"Ja," the bishop replied simply.

The tears spilled over. She covered her face with her hands. *"Danke, Gott, danke,"* she whispered between heaving breaths. His throat closed at the intensity of her emotion.

Then it struck him. Abigail could be baptized. That meant...

Benjamin looked over at the bishop, who was watching him as if reading his thoughts. The older man smiled, then nodded.

Benjamin's own breath caught. Suddenly, urgently, he wanted the bishop to leave. He had some things to discuss with the woman sitting across from him, the woman he hoped would be around forever.

"So I wanted to ask you both to forgive this old man," concluded the bishop. "I was a fool, and I'm sorry for it."

Abigail continued to weep. Benjamin fished a clean handkerchief from his pocket and handed it to her. She nodded blindly and buried her face in it.

But when she raised her head at last, her eyes were red and her cheeks were blotchy, but her face shone with a radiant joy he had never seen before. "All is forgiven," she choked.

"*Ja,*" croaked Benjamin. "All is forgiven."

Bishop Beiler pushed away his untouched glass of lemonade and rose from the table. "Then I'll go home now," he said. "Lois will be anxious to know what happened to Thomasina, and I have a lot to tell her. And I think," he added with a twinkle in his eyes, "you two have much to talk about."

Chapter Sixteen

The sounds of the horse's hooves faded in the distance as Abigail wiped her eyes. "I can be baptized," she murmured. It still seemed too good to be true.

"Abigail." Benjamin, sitting across the small porch table from her, laid both his hands palm up on the table. "If you can be baptized, you know what this means."

The full realization came over her like a thunderclap. "Oh, Benjamin…" She laid her hands in his. "Is it true? Can this happen?"

"I will ask you again. Will you let me court you?" His face was solemn.

She managed a chuckle through her tears. "Let's just say you've been doing that since the day I arrived. Ask me something else."

"All right." He smiled, and the glint in his

dark blue eyes held a promise of the future. "Here's my next question. Will you marry me?"

"Ja." Though she smiled, she couldn't prevent another tear from trickling down her cheek. *"Ja,* I will marry you, as *Gott* is my witness."

He closed his eyes as if in prayer. "As *Gott* is my witness," he breathed.

"But it can't be right away," she warned. "I have to go through the usual five months of instruction before baptism. But, conveniently, that puts my baptism in November, just in time for wedding season."

"And if you're baptized on a Sabbath, then we can have the wedding the following Tuesday or Thursday." He grinned.

"In a hurry, are you?" she teased.

"Let's just say I'd marry you tomorrow, if I could get away with it."

But despite the unsteady golden happiness she felt—and she knew Benjamin felt—she knew she had some serious issues to bring up.

"Benjamin…" She paused and bit her lip. "Before we go any further, you need to be aware of something. You're not asking a normal Amish woman to be your wife. I'll be working. Will that be all right?"

"Ja, sure…"

She waved a hand. "Don't answer so quickly.

It's worth thinking through. You once mentioned you weren't much of a cook. If I'm working full-time, I won't be much of a cook, either. And it's not just kitchen duties, it's everything. Are you sure you can accept that?"

"Ja." He smiled, apparently not put off in the slightest by her litany of warnings. "Believe me, Abigail, I've thought everything through from one side to the other, from beginning to end, from left to right, up and down, in and out, and every other direction you can think of. Nothing you can say can deter me from marrying you."

She shook her head. "You're giddy, Benjamin. So am I. But we have to be realistic." She drew a deep breath. *"Mamm* asked me this morning to imagine a situation. She asked if I could be happy scaling back to part-time work, or even volunteer work, when babies started coming. I—I think I can. Obviously there will be times I won't be able to work at all. Other times I might be able to work part-time…"

"I think you're overthinking this," he interrupted, still smiling. "I may not be much of a cook, but you know what? I'm great with kids. *Ja*, there may be times you'll have a new baby when you may not be able to work. But it's a stage of life, Abigail. However many *bopplin Gott* gives us remains to be seen, but *Gott* willing, you and I will have many, many years ahead of us. When the *kinner* are older, I can take care of them full-time."

"You would do that for me?"

"*Ja*. I would do that for you." His eyes glinted. "I might even put that in our wedding vows."

She felt like laughing and crying at the same time. The laughter spilled out, and he joined her. For a moment she was dazzled at the prospect of laughing with this wonderful man for the rest of her life.

"And when the *kinner* are grown and no longer live with us, then you can take care of animals full-time, if you want," Benjamin said.

She grew sober. "I'll have to see if John Green, the vet, can accept my application under those conditions. There are times I may need to reduce my hours to an emergency basis only. He may not want to hire me if those are my conditions."

"And if not, then what?"

She sniffed and smiled at him. "Then it's what *Mamm* suggested. I may simply have to be an independent freelancer working just within the Amish community, doing what I can. Anything I can't do without the right equipment, I'll refer to the clinic. Oh, Benjamin, I think this might work!"

"You're right. We may not live a typical Amish life, but we'll *make* it work." He held out his arms. "Come here."

"I'm filthy." She indicated her stained apron and dress.

"What does it matter? Soon you'll be wearing a brand-new clean dress for our wedding. Come here."

Suddenly shy, she rose and walked around the table and perched herself on his lap. He touched his forehead to hers. "I never thought this day would come," he murmured, and kissed her.

She returned the kiss and tasted the promise of a long and happy future with her soon-to-be husband.

A few minutes later she pulled back. "Now, what's this about you pleading my case with the bishop? I didn't know that."

She felt the rumble of laughter start deep in his chest. "Call it an act of desperation. I went and talked with him this morning, asking if he could find clemency in his heart for your situation. And for mine, too. I told him I wanted to court you, but he said the decision was up to you—about whether you could give up being a veterinarian. I must admit, I went away a little huffy."

"What a difference a few hours makes." She

sighed with happiness, then a thought struck her. "If you have a puppy to spare, perhaps you should offer one to the bishop. It seems his farm could use a livestock guard dog."

"*Ja*, perhaps. I'll ask if he's interested. This litter is spoken for, but perhaps next year."

"Next year," she breathed. Tucked against Benjamin's chest, she could see the view from the porch—green lawn, dark conifers, distant mountains. "Next year, we'll both be living in this lovely little cabin. Perhaps we'll have a *boppli* by then. Oh, Benjamin, I love you."

His arms tightened around her fractionally. Then abruptly he sat up, nearly unseating her from his lap. "I think now would be a *gut* time to give you your wedding present."

"My what?"

He lifted her off his lap and stood up. "Stay here a moment."

"What are you talking about? How could you possibly have a wedding present for me?"

He grinned. "Let's just say I was hopeful." He gently pushed her down into the porch rocker. "Close your eyes. I'll be back in a moment."

She closed her eyes. The day had been such an emotional seesaw that somehow Benjamin's silly announcement of a present was just another part of that.

She heard him come back onto the porch. "Hold out your hands. Both hands," he instructed.

She did so, and a moment later felt the soft, warm body of a puppy fill her arms. Instinctively she embraced it while her eyes popped open. "Benjamin! The puppy!"

"Ja." With a grin as wide as the porch, he sat back down. "He's yours. Literally from the moment he was born, when you brought him back to life, I earmarked him for you. I was hoping to give him to you as a wedding gift. *Gott* granted me that wish."

She sniffed back more tears and hugged the animal against her chest. "*Danke*, Benjamin. He's beautiful. I'll have to think of a name for him."

"Goliath, perhaps? He's likely to be huge."

"I like it." She held the puppy up at eye level. "Hello, Goliath. How would you like to stay here with us?" The baby responded by touching her nose with his tongue. "Will he be a field guardian or a house dog?" she wondered.

"Whichever you prefer," Benjamin replied. "If you want him as a house dog, we'll have to put a fence around the yard or he'll roam. All Pyrenees need space—they're not meant to be confined—so I can make it a good-size yard."

"He can guard our *kinner*!" She hugged the dog to her chest.

Benjamin nodded with more gravity than she anticipated. "And believe me, he will. Pyrenees take their job seriously." He glanced upward at the porch roof. "I'll have to expand this house," he said thoughtfully. "It's fine for two people, but I suspect we won't be two people for very long."

"It's such a beautiful, classic log cabin," she replied. "Hopefully you can make whatever additions we'll need without changing the look too much."

"I have some ideas." He grinned at her. "I've had ideas ever since you arrived just in time to set Lydia's leg. I think I started falling in love with you from that moment on."

"It didn't take me long to return the notice," she admitted. "I was just so tied up in knots. Now it seems everything is simple and easy, even though, as I said before, we're bound to have an unconventional lifestyle." She put the wiggly puppy down on the porch. "And we won't ever have to separate Goliath from his mother…" She jerked upright. "Mother! Benjamin, *Mamm* has no idea what's happened! She doesn't know that the bishop's cat survived, or that the bishop changed his mind about my baptism, or that we'll be courting."

He smiled. "What do you say we go see her and drop all the bombshells on her at once? Won't that be fun?"

"Ja!" Giggling, she scooped up Goliath and redeposited him back among his siblings. Then she grabbed Benjamin's hand. "Race you!"

Epilogue

November in the Rockies, Abigail realized, was very different than November in Indiana. The season's first snow had capped the distant mountains and dusted the nearby conifers with what looked like powdered sugar. The air was crisp and clean, and smelled of pine.

"I'm so glad the weather held," observed Esther from the back of the buggy.

Abigail, attired in her newly made blue dress with clean black apron, turned to look at her mother. "Is this the first wedding to take place here in Pierce?"

"*Nein*, it's the third," her mother answered. "No one has a house big enough to host a wedding, so the Millers' bed-and-breakfast has become the preferred spot."

"And all of Abigail's coworkers will attend as well, even though this is a Thursday," added Benjamin, guiding the horse onto the paved road.

Many Amish buggies were heading into town, causing heads to turn. John Green, her boss, had said the community was welcome to park as many buggies as could fit into the vet clinic's parking lot, located only a block away from the Millers' bed-and-breakfast. John had closed the office for the day so the entire veterinary staff could attend her wedding. She had warned him in advance the service would be in German.

She hugged herself, then glanced over at the man who would be her husband within a few hours. As if feeling her gaze, he looked over at her, winked and smiled. His dark blue eyes were warm with love.

Trying not to become overwhelmed with emotion, she thought back over the last week. On Sunday she had been baptized, and she was now a full-fledged member of the church. Esther had wept with joy that her youngest child had returned to the fold, just as she had wept with joy five months before, when Abigail had told her she and Benjamin were to be married.

The bishop's cat, Thomasina, had actually been present at the baptismal ceremony at Abigail's request. The feline had completely recuperated and was extremely fond of her, and had taken the unorthodox approach of sleeping in Abigail's lap during the subsequent sermon. It was not a common sight to see a cat at a Sabbath service, but the bishop had been indulgent.

And Goliath. She smiled at the thought of her gigantic puppy, now nearly six months old and already seventy pounds. He was likely to top out at a massive 150 pounds at full maturity, like his sire. She made sure he was well socialized both with other dogs, as well as people. He adored her as much as she adored him.

But most of all, there was Benjamin. Her soon-to-be husband had changed over the last five months. Whereas before he had been something of a loner, and had times of bitterness or recrimination—an "odd duck," as Esther once described him—he had transformed into a calm and cheerful man, one whose smile seemed never to leave his face. His furniture business and the constant orders from the log-cabin builder had stabilized into steady work that Benjamin could handle by himself.

She remembered Eva's words when describing her marriage with Daniel: "He's everything I could hope for in a *hutband*. I try to be everything he could hope for in a wife."

That's what Abigail wanted to be—everything Benjamin could hope for in a wife.

Benjamin guided the horse to the front of the Millers' B and B, then alighted to assist his bride and his future mother-in-law from the buggy. "I'll be back in a moment," he told her, then swung back into the seat of the vehicle to park it behind the vet clinic.

John Green, her boss, stood near the door of the building. Near him was the clinic staff—the vets, the techs, the administrators. Abigail had become close to her coworkers in the last few months.

"Your big day!" John exclaimed, clasping her hands.

"Ja." She smiled at her boss. "And I couldn't be happier."

She entered the building and seated herself in the front row as the bridal party began assembling. Benjamin came in, flanked by his groomsmen, and sat next to her. He snuck his hand around hers. She twined her fingers with his.

The service started with traditional wedding hymns, and Bishop Beiler's sermon on the importance of marriage as a covenant before *Gott.*

And when at last the bishop asked her and

Benjamin to rise and stand before him, Benjamin refused to let go of her hand.

"You're stuck with me now," he whispered.

She quirked a smile at him. "We're stuck with each other," she whispered back. *"Gott ist gut."*

* * * * *

*If you enjoyed this story,
look for Patrice Lewis's earlier books:*

The Amish Newcomer
Amish Baby Lessons
Her Path to Redemption

Available now from Love Inspired!

*Find more great reads at
www.LoveInspired.com*

Dear Reader,

A few years ago, I lost a beloved dog. Her name was Lydia and she was a beautiful Great Pyrenees. What a joy it was to bring her back to life within the pages of this book.

While I've never studied animal medicine, I've spent much of my life studying animals. When I was a kid, I wanted to be just like Jane Goodall. I majored in zoology in college. I worked as a field biologist for a long time. Today I spend my time caring for livestock and admiring the abundant wildlife that graces our rural valley. I have enormous sympathy for my heroine, Abigail, who must balance her God-given affinity for animals with her spiritual needs.

I hope you enjoyed reading *The Amish Animal Doctor*. I love hearing from readers, so feel free to email me at patricelewis1305@mail.com.

Patrice

Get 4 FREE REWARDS!

We'll send you 2 FREE Books **plus** 2 FREE Mystery Gifts.

FREE
Value Over
$20

Both the **Love Inspired®** and **Love Inspired® Suspense** series feature compelling novels filled with inspirational romance, faith, forgiveness, and hope.

YES! Please send me 2 FREE novels from the Love Inspired or Love Inspired Suspense series and my 2 FREE gifts (gifts are worth about $10 retail). After receiving them, if I don't wish to receive any more books, I can return the shipping statement marked "cancel." If I don't cancel, I will receive 6 brand-new Love Inspired Larger-Print books or Love Inspired Suspense Larger-Print books every month and be billed just $5.99 each in the U.S. or $6.24 each in Canada. That is a savings of at least 17% off the cover price. It's quite a bargain! Shipping and handling is just 50¢ per book in the U.S. and $1.25 per book in Canada.* I understand that accepting the 2 free books and gifts places me under no obligation to buy anything. I can always return a shipment and cancel at any time. The free books and gifts are mine to keep no matter what I decide.

Choose one: ☐ **Love Inspired**
Larger-Print
(122/322 IDN GNWC)

☐ **Love Inspired Suspense**
Larger-Print
(107/307 IDN GNWN)

Name (please print)

Address   Apt. #

City   State/Province   Zip/Postal Code

Email: Please check this box ☐ if you would like to receive newsletters and promotional emails from Harlequin Enterprises ULC and its affiliates. You can unsubscribe anytime.

Mail to the Harlequin Reader Service:
IN U.S.A.: P.O. Box 1341, Buffalo, NY 14240-8531
IN CANADA: P.O. Box 603, Fort Erie, Ontario L2A 5X3

Want to try 2 free books from another series! Call 1-800-873-8635 or visit www.ReaderService.com.

*Terms and prices subject to change without notice. Prices do not include sales taxes, which will be charged (if applicable) based on your state or country of residence. Canadian residents will be charged applicable taxes. Offer not valid in Quebec. This offer is limited to one order per household. Books received may not be as shown. Not valid for current subscribers to the Love Inspired or Love Inspired Suspense series. All orders subject to approval. Credit or debit balances in a customer's account(s) may be offset by any other outstanding balance owed by or to the customer. Please allow 4 to 6 weeks for delivery. Offer available while quantities last.

Your Privacy—Your information is being collected by Harlequin Enterprises ULC, operating as Harlequin Reader Service. For a complete summary of the information we collect, how we use this information and to whom it is disclosed, please visit our privacy notice located at corporate.harlequin.com/privacy-notice. From time to time we may also exchange your personal information with reputable third parties. If you wish to opt out of this sharing of your personal information, please visit readerservice.com/consumerchoice or call 1-800-873-8635. **Notice to California Residents**—Under California law, you have specific rights to control and access your data. For more information on these rights and how to exercise them, visit corporate.harlequin.com/california-privacy.

LIRLIS22

Get 4 FREE REWARDS!

We'll send you 2 FREE Books plus 2 FREE Mystery Gifts.

FREE Value Over **$20**

Both the **Harlequin® Special Edition** and **Harlequin® Heartwarming™** series feature compelling novels filled with stories of love and strength where the bonds of friendship, family and community unite.

YES! Please send me 2 FREE novels from the Harlequin Special Edition or Harlequin Heartwarming series and my 2 FREE gifts (gifts are worth about $10 retail). After receiving them, if I don't wish to receive any more books, I can return the shipping statement marked "cancel." If I don't cancel, I will receive 6 brand-new Harlequin Special Edition books every month and be billed just $4.99 each in the U.S or $5.74 each in Canada, a savings of at least 17% off the cover price or 4 brand-new Harlequin Heartwarming Larger-Print books every month and be billed just $5.74 each in the U.S. or $6.24 each in Canada, a savings of at least 21% off the cover price. It's quite a bargain! Shipping and handling is just 50¢ per book in the U.S. and $1.25 per book in Canada.* I understand that accepting the 2 free books and gifts places me under no obligation to buy anything. I can always return a shipment and cancel at any time. The free books and gifts are mine to keep no matter what I decide.

Choose one: ☐ **Harlequin Special Edition**
(235/335 HDN GNMP) ☐ **Harlequin Heartwarming
Larger-Print**
(161/361 HDN GNPZ)

Name (please print)

Address   Apt. #

City   State/Province   Zip/Postal Code

Email: Please check this box ☐ if you would like to receive newsletters and promotional emails from Harlequin Enterprises ULC and its affiliates. You can unsubscribe anytime.

Mail to the **Harlequin Reader Service:**
IN U.S.A.: P.O. Box 1341, Buffalo, NY 14240-8531
IN CANADA: P.O. Box 603, Fort Erie, Ontario L2A 5X3

Want to try 2 free books from another series! Call 1-800-873-8635 or visit www.ReaderService.com.

---

*Terms and prices subject to change without notice. Prices do not include sales taxes, which will be charged (if applicable) based on your state or country of residence. Canadian residents will be charged applicable taxes. Offer not valid in Quebec. This offer is limited to one order per household. Books received may not be as shown. Not valid for current subscribers to the Harlequin Special Edition or Harlequin Heartwarming series. All orders subject to approval. Credit or debit balances in a customer's account(s) may be offset by any other outstanding balance owed by or to the customer. Please allow 4 to 6 weeks for delivery. Offer available while quantities last.

Your Privacy—Your information is being collected by Harlequin Enterprises ULC, operating as Harlequin Reader Service. For a complete summary of the information we collect, how we use this information and to whom it is disclosed, please visit our privacy notice located at corporate.harlequin.com/privacy-notice. From time to time we may also exchange your personal information with reputable third parties. If you wish to opt out of this sharing of your personal information, please visit readerservice.com/consumerschoice or call 1-800-873-8635. **Notice to California Residents**—Under California law, you have specific rights to control and access your data. For more information on these rights and how to exercise them, visit corporate.harlequin.com/california-privacy.

HSEHW22

COUNTRY LEGACY COLLECTION

19 FREE BOOKS IN ALL!

Cowboys, adventure and romance await you in this new collection! Enjoy superb reading all year long with books by bestselling authors like Diana Palmer, Sasha Summers and Marie Ferrarella!